CRITICAL ACCLAIM

'Parker writes old-time, stri_ _ _ _ _ _ _ _ _ _ _ _, hard-boiled school of Chandler… His novels are funny, smart and highly entertaining… There's no writer I'd rather take on an aeroplane'
– *Sunday Telegraph*

'Parker packs more meaning into a whispered "yeah" than most writers can pack into a page'
– *Sunday Times*

'Why Robert Parker's not better known in Britain is a mystery. His best series featuring Boston-based PI Spenser is a triumph of style and substance'
– *Daily Mirror*

'Robert B. Parker is one of the greats of the American hard-boiled genre'
– *Guardian*

'Nobody does it better than Parker…'
– *Sunday Times*

'Parker's sentences flow with as much wit, grace and assurance as ever, and Stone is a complex and consistently interesting new protagonist'
– *Newsday*

'If Robert B. Parker doesn't blow it, in the new series he set up in *Night Passage* and continues with *Trouble in Paradise*, he could go places and take the kind of risks that wouldn't be seemly in his popular Spenser stories'
– **Marilyn Stasio**, *New York Times*

THE SPENSER NOVELS

The Godwulf Manuscript
God Save the Child
Mortal Stakes
Promised Land
The Judas Goat
Looking for Rachel Wallace
Early Autumn
A Savage Place
Ceremony
The Widening Gyre
Valediction
A Catskill Eagle
Taming a Sea-Horse
Pale Kings and Princes
Crimson Joy
Playmates
Stardust
Pastime
Double Deuce
Paper Doll
Walking Shadow
Thin Air

Chance
Small Vices*
Sudden Mischief*
Hush Money*
Hugger Mugger*
Potshot*
Widow's Walk*
Back Story*
Bad Business*
Cold Service*
School Days*
Dream Girl
  (aka Hundred-Dollar Baby)*
Now & Then*
Rough Weather
The Professional
Painted Ladies
Sixkill
Lullaby (by Ace Atkins)
Wonderland (by Ace Atkins)*
Silent Night (by Helen Brann)*
Cheap Shot*

THE JESSE STONE MYSTERIES

Night Passage*
Trouble in Paradise*
Death in Paradise*
Stone Cold*
Sea Change*
High Profile*
Stranger in Paradise
Night and Day

Split Image
Fool Me Twice (by Michael Brandman)
Killing the Blues (by Michael
  Brandman)
**Damned If You Do (by Michael
  Brandman)***
Blind Spot*

THE SUNNY RANDALL MYSTERIES

Family Honor*
Perish Twice*
Shrink Rap*

Melancholy Baby*
Blue Screen*
Spare Change*

ALSO BY ROBERT B. PARKER

Training with Weights
(with John R. Marsh)
Three Weeks in Spring
(with Joan Parker)
Wilderness
Love and Glory
Poodle Springs
(and Raymond Chandler)
Perchance to Dream

A Year at the Races (with Joan Parker)
All Our Yesterdays
Gunman's Rhapsody
Double Play*
Appaloosa
Resolution
Brimstone
Blue Eyed Devil
Ironhorse (by Robert Knott)

***Available from No Exit Press**

ROBERT B. PARKER
DOUBLE PLAY

NO EXIT PRESS

This edition published 2015
by No Exit Press,
an imprint of Oldcastle Books
P.O.Box 394, Harpenden,
Herts, AL5 1XJ

A portion of this work first appeared in 'Harlem Nocarne' in Murders' Row, edited by Otto Penzler, New Millennium Press ©2001 Robert B. Parker

A CIP catalogue record for this book is available from the British Library.

ISBN
978-1-84344-440-4 (print)
978-1- 84344-324-7 (epub)
978-1- 84344-325-4 (kindle)
978-1- 84344-326-1 (pdf)

4 6 8 10 9 7 5 3

Typeset in 11.25pt Minion
by Avocet Typeset, Somerton, Somerset
Printed and bound by CPI Group (UK) Ltd, Croydon, CR0 4YY

For Joan, who has, as I suspect of Rachel Robinson,
made all the difference

NOTE

This is a work of fiction about a real man. Most of what I've written I made up. I have, however, attempted to render Jackie Robinson accurately. As he was, or as I imagined him to be, in 1947, when I was turning fifteen, and he was changing the world. The rest is altogether fiction. It may be more Burke's story than Jackie's. But without Jackie, Burke would have had no story. And neither would I.

Robert B. Parker
Cambridge, Massachusetts
June 2003

1

Joseph Burke got it on Guadalcanal, at Bloody Ridge, five .25 caliber slugs from a Jap light machine gun, stitched across him in a neatly punctuated line. The medics put on pressure bandages and shot him up with morphine and nothing much made any sense to him afterward. It was a blur of tubes and nurses and bright lights and descents into darkness, surgeons, frightening visions, and bad smells and the feel of ocean. One day he looked around and he was in bed in a hospital.

'Where the fuck am I?' he asked a nurse.

'Chelsea Naval Hospital.'

'Am I going to live?' he said.

She was a fat gray-haired woman with deep circles under her eyes. She nodded.

'Yes,' she said.

For weeks he was paranoid delusional. He heard the nurses whispering together at night. They had husbands in the army; they hated Marines. He could hear their husbands whispering with them, visiting them on the floor, parking their cars with the motors running just outside his window. The ceiling lights were recessed. He saw small figures in them, a man being greeted by a butler in an ornate hallway. He slept only in moments, watching the clock on the ward wall. 0300 hours. Dawn will be here in 180 minutes. He could see the tip of a steeple through the window on the opposite wall. Sometimes he thought it was the bridge of a troop ship. Sometimes he thought it was the church he used to go to in South Boston. Sometimes it was a church steeple outside his hospital window. His wife came to visit. He asked her if she would bring him a gun, it would make him feel safer. If he had a gun he wouldn't feel so scared. One day they disconnected him from his tubes and one of the nurses got him up and helped him walk the length of the ward. He had to sit for a while in a straight chair at the other end, before he made the return trip. The next time they took him for a short walk into the corridor, past the nurses' station to the visitors' lounge. He walked stoop-shouldered, shuffling his feet. He sat in the lounge for a while with a small red-haired nurse with freckles. Then he shuffled back. At night he woke up and heard the nurses plotting with their boyfriends, the engines of their parked cars murmuring outside his window. He mentioned it the next morning to a nurse.

'Cars with their motors running?' the nurse said.

'Yeah. I keep listening to them. I keep hoping that they'll leave, but they don't.'

'Right outside the window?'

'Yeah.'

'You're on the ninth floor.'

He heard her but the words meant nothing.

'Too many drugs,' the nurse said. 'Too long in the intensive care unit. It's making you crazy.'

He knew she was right. He knew he was crazy, but oddly, knowing it didn't make him less crazy. Sometimes he knew both realities at the same time. He knew he was in a ward at the Chelsea Naval Hospital. He also knew he was being stalked in a stark diner in New Bedford on a bitter cold night. His wife hadn't brought him the gun. He wasn't sure if she'd come back again.

They had him walking every day now. One day he made it, round trip – to the end of the ward and back – without stopping to rest. One day they brought him solid food. A ham sandwich on white bread. He couldn't eat it. They brought it again the next day. He took a bite but couldn't force himself to swallow. When no one was looking he spit it into a bedpan. One day a physical therapy nurse came and took him for a walk out of the ward. They went past the visitors' lounge to a stairwell.

'We'll just try a couple of stairs,' the nurse said.

He walked up two and, clinging to the railing, walked back down. After that she came every day and took him to the stairs. One day he made the full flight. He drank a little soup. One of the doctors came and examined his wounds, sniffing them to see if they smelled of infection. In a few days the doctor came back and took out the stitches.

The red-haired nurse walked with him, a hand on his arm, when he came out of the hospital and got into a cab. She helped him into the cab and the cab took him home.

The cabbie carried his duffel to the front door of the second-floor apartment. Dragging it inside exhausted him. His wife wasn't there. He sat for a while on the wing chair near the front door, and then stood and walked slowly through the apartment to their bedroom. Her clothes were gone. He went slowly to the bathroom. Her toothbrush was not there. Her makeup was gone. With one hand on the wall he trudged to the kitchen. The refrigerator was empty. He sat on a chair in the tiny kitchen and rested. Then he stood effortfully and went slowly back to the living room. He sat on the couch. He put his head back against the cushions and closed his eyes. Silent. He opened his eyes and looked at the living room. Empty. On the coffee table was an envelope with his name on it. He knew her handwriting. He looked at the envelope for a while. He had so little energy that all his reactions were slow, and everything he did was languid. He picked up the envelope and opened it. He held the letter a moment while he rested. Then he unfolded the letter.

'I'm sorry,' the letter said. 'I wanted to tell you the day I came to the hospital. But you were so sick. I couldn't.'

He rested the letter on his thigh for a moment and took in some air.

'While you were gone, I met somebody. Somebody I must be with. I'm sorry. I will always care for you. But I've got to be with him.'

She was never much of a letter writer. Not much of a wife either. He put his head back against the cushions of the couch and closed his eyes and heard himself breathing.

PENTIMENTO

What he remembered most about her was that she almost never wore stockings. He always remembered that when he thought of her. Her name was Carole Duke. In his mind she always looked the same. Dark blue dress with tiny white polka dots, hair worn short, like Claudette Colbert, carefully shaven legs white and stockingless, red high heels. He knew she wore many other things, and no things, but he always remembered her that way.

He met Carole at a USO, in the Back Bay, near Kenmore Square. He was eighteen, on leave between boot camp and the Pacific, at loose ends. His father had died the previous summer in a construction accident. His mother didn't seem to him like a mother. She seemed to him like a drunken slattern, so while everybody else went home after basic, he rented a room, and drifted around the city, waiting until it was time to ship out. He didn't feel particularly lonely. He missed his father, but his mother had ceased to matter a long time ago.

At the USO there was food and big band music, and hostesses who volunteered to dance with the young servicemen soon to be in combat. The room was full of men in uniform. One of the young women, a hostess wearing a blue dress with white polka dots, spoke to him.

'Want to dance, Marine?'

He said he did. And they swung out onto the dance floor to 'American Patrol.'

'So where are you from, Mr Marine?'

'Boston,' he said.

'Home on leave?'

'Sort of.'

'Sort of?'

He told her that his mother lived here but they didn't get along. He told her he had rented a room on Huntington Avenue.

'You have your orders yet?' she said.

The band played 'There Are Such Things,' and they slowed. She pressed herself against him.

'First Marines,' he said.

'Sounds like the Pacific to me,' she said.

'Yes.'

Her face was near his as they danced. She smelled like good soap.

'Wow,' she said. 'I'd be so scared.'

'I guess I'll be scared,' he said. 'I guess everybody is.'

'But you do it.'

'Sure.'

'That's so brave,' she said.

He pressed his hand into the small of her back as they danced. A female vocalist sang, 'I don't want to walk without you, baby...'

'And you have no one to worry about you?'

'I'll worry about me,' he said.

She laughed softly. He could feel her breath on his neck.

'Well, dammit,' she said. 'I will, too.'

She had an apartment on Park Drive not far from the Harvard Medical School area where she worked. He looked around: small foyer, living room on the right, bath next to it, bedroom on the left, tiny kitchen ahead.

'You got your own apartment?' he said.

'Sure.'

'You live alone here?'

'Yes. Why?'

'I been living in a barracks with a lot of guys. Alone seems nice.'

'As long as it's not too alone,' she said. 'Would you like a drink?'

'Sure.'

She brought out some Vat 69 scotch and some ice and a glass siphon with a lacy silver design on it. She poured two scotches, added some ice, and squirted the carbonated water from the siphon. She handed him one.

'Come on, Mr Marine, sit with me on the couch.'

He sat. She sat beside him. Her bare legs gleamed. He drank some scotch. It was good. His drinking experience was mostly beer up till now.

'How old are you?' she said.

'Eighteen.'

He almost called her ma'am, but caught himself.

'Wow,' she said, 'I'm twenty-five.'

He didn't know what to say about this, so he simply nodded.

'What do you think about that?' she said.

'Doesn't seem to matter,' he said.

'No,' she said. 'It doesn't seem to.'

'Were you in high school until the Marines?' she said.

'No. I quit school,' he said. 'I was doing high ironwork, with a bunch of Mohawk Indians.'

'High iron?'

'Yeah, you know, skyscrapers. Mostly the Mohawks do that stuff, but they needed a guy quick, and I was willing.'

'My God,' she said.

'You get used to it,' he said. 'My father did it too.'

'And you don't get along with your mother?'

'No,' he said.

'Because?'

He could feel the length of her thigh against his as she sat beside him.

'A lot of booze,' he said. 'A lot of men,'

'How awful,' she said.

He shrugged.

'She does what she does,' he said. 'I do what I do.'

She shifted on the couch and tucked her bare legs beneath her and turned toward him, holding the glass of scotch in both hands.

'And what do you do?' she said.

'Lately,' he said, 'I been learning to shoot a rifle.'

'There are better things,' she said.

12

'Not where I'm going.'

She smiled.

'No, but you're not there yet.'

He nodded. They were close now, and carefully he put his arm around her. She rested her head against his shoulder.

'You may be young but you seem awfully big and strong,' she said.

'High iron does that,' he said. 'You should have seen my father.'

'I should,' she said. 'Could you talk to him?'

'Yes.'

'But not your mother.'

'No.'

'So you're going off to war with no one to talk to?'

'I'm talking to you,' he said.

'But you must have a lot of feelings bundled up in there,' she said. 'You need to be able to let go, let it all out.'

'Marines mostly teach you to shut up about stuff,' he said.

'Well, I will teach you differently,' she said. 'Have you ever had intercourse?'

He was silent for a moment. His impulse was to claim that he had, but there was something here, something between them. He didn't want to lie.

'No,' he said. 'I haven't.'

'Then it's time,' she said and leaned toward him and kissed him on the mouth.

Bobby

In the summer of 1941, when I was nine, my father used to work around the yard on Sunday afternoons wearing a white undershirt and bear pants. The bear pants were over washed khakis that he was wearing when, as a young man in Maine, he had shot a bear. The bear's blood still stained the pants, and they became known as the bear pants. The bear pants were, for me, though I would not have known how to say it, totemic, the tangible vestige of a warrior past no longer available.

We lived ninety miles west of Boston, in Springfield, in a white house with a screened back porch. My father used to play the radio loudly on the porch while he worked in the garden or clipped the hedge, so he could listen to the ball game. There were still blue laws in Boston in the days before the war, and baseball was not broadcast on Sundays. So while he staked his tomato plants and weeded among his string beans, my father listened to the Brooklyn Dodgers on WHN, which came clear channel up the Connecticut River Valley from New York.

Normally on Sundays teams played a double header, so all the slow summer afternoon I would hear Red Barber's play-by-play with Connie Desmond, until the sound of it became the lullaby of summer, a song sung in unison with my father. I saw Ebbets Field in my imagination long before I ever saw the bricks and mortar. Therotunda, the right field screen with Bedford Avenue behind it. Schaefer Beer, Old Gold cigarettes, the scoreboard and Abe Stark's sign. Brooklyn itself became a place of exotica and excitement for me, and the perfumed allure of New York City, gleaming between its rivers, wafted up the Connecticut Valley and lingered in my nostrils as it has lingered since, years before my father took me there and I found, to my adolescent delight, that it was what I'd imagined.

I learned something of triumph when the Dodgers won the National League pennant in 1941. I did not know who won in 1940. I learned years later that it was Cincinnati. I did not know any players in 1940. By the time I was nine, in September of 1941, the names of the Dodgers marched through my mind like lyrics: Dolph Camelli, Billy Herman, Pee Wee Reese, Cookie Lavagetto, Ducky Medwick, Pete Reiser, Dixie Walker, Mickey Owen. The pitchers: Higbe and Wyatt and Hugh Casey. And I learned something about tragedy in the World Series when Mickey Owen missed the third strike on Tommy Henrich to give the Yankees another chance to win, which they did. I regret it still.

Listening to the scores – Pittsburgh 4, Chicago 2; Cleveland 8, Detroit 1 – I felt connected to all the great cities I'd never seen, across the vast rolling reaches of the Republic, connecting me with them and the people there watching the games. I saw them. I smelled the steamy heat in their streets. Philadelphia, Washington, Cincinnati.

In that last summer before the war, listening to the radio while my father wore his bear pants and worked in the yard, it was as if I learned the shaman incantations of a magic sect. The sound of the bat, amplified by the crowd mike. The call of the vendors, the organ playing, the sound of the fans yelling things you could never quite make out. The effortless and certain cadences of the play-by-play announcers, all of it became like the sound of a mother's heart-beat to her unborn child, the rhythm of life and certainty. The sound of permanence.

When my father was through working he'd have a beer, Ballantine as I recall, and he'd pour some in a shot glass and say to me, 'Want a drink, Bob?'

It was, for me, the potion of initiation. Women didn't drink beer and listen to ball games on summer afternoons, and they didn't wear bear pants.

2

For more than a month he was too weak to do anything except sit in a chair near the window and look at what was happening on the street. He had some mustering-out pay left, and several times a week a home worker from the VA came around and brought him some groceries. Most of them went unused. He couldn't eat. It wasn't even that food repelled him. He simply didn't want it and couldn't force himself to eat it. He drank a little soup most days. And sometimes a half a slice of toast. The home worker brought him books and magazines but he didn't have the energy to read. He listened to the radio. He slept part of the day. Nights were difficult. The visiting nurse came once a week. The scars on his stomach and chest were still bright, but there was no infection. He hadn't smoked since he was wounded. He couldn't stand to drink coffee. On her third weekly visit the nurse took him for a walk to the corner of his block and back. He walked like an elderly man, his shoulders forward, taking small shuffling steps, shivering. The weather was mild, and he was bundled up, but he was cold. He stopped at the corner, and turned and looked back at the insurmountable distance back down his block.

'You can make it,' the nurse said.

She was a fat young woman with long black hair and an Irish face. Her name was Madeline Murphy.

'It'll get easier as time goes by,' she said. 'Once your blood count gets back up.'

Burke nodded. They began to slowly walk back.

'So, what are your plans?' Madeline said. 'After you get back on your feet.'

Burke shook his head.

'You don't know?' Madeline said. 'Or you won't tell?'

'Don't know,' Burke said.

'Well, what are you trained for?' Madeline said.

It seemed to Burke that they were no closer to his place than they had been. He glanced over at Madeline and smiled a little.

'Rifleman,' he said.

Carole was helpful, he remembered, but not managerial. He was tentative. She was patient. He hurried. She patted him gently.

'Just let it happen,' she murmured, 'people know how to do this at birth, just let it happen.'

He could feel himself loosen, feel the rhythm of it, feel himself expand and intensify, feel his existence narrow to her face, just below him, her eyes very wide.

'Let it come, Marine,' she murmured, 'let everything come.'

It was his first time. He didn't last long. As he ejaculated he hugged her so hard she could barely breathe.

'Everything,' she murmured, 'everything.'

He began to cry, gasping for breath as the sobs racked him, his body shaking. Eventually he slowed, and finally he lay still against her, his face against her naked breast. He cried softly. She kept her arms around him and patted.

'It's all right,' she said. 'I'm here. You're here with me. It's all right.'

'Can I stay with you?' he said.

'Of course,' she said and patted him some more. 'Of course.'

He kept his head against her. She smelled of soap and perfume, and something else, something female and alive. Like her bare legs, he would always remember how she smelled.

They were quiet like that, lying in her bed, in the small apartment, on the second floor, with the air stirring through the open window enough to stir the curtains.

'I feel funny about crying,' he said.

'No need.'

'Men shouldn't cry.'

'Of course they should,' she said. 'They cry all the time.'

'You're the first woman...'

'I know,' she said. 'It's been all men, and high places, and not being afraid. No softness. No love.'

'My father loved me,' Burke said.

'Not like a woman,' she said.

'No,' he said. 'Not like that.'

'With a woman you needn't pretend,' she said. 'You can be whatever you are.'

'I guess so,' Burke said. 'Can we have intercourse again?'

'Of course,' she said. 'Of course we can.'

Bobby

I actually turned nine in September of 1941.

In the early winter of that year, my father picked me up at the movies in our 1939 Plymouth. On the ride home he told me that the Japanese had bombed Pearl Harbor, and we were at war. He was quite formal about it, 'the Japanese' he said. Thereafter for the next four years they would be Japs.

I was thrilled. Ever since the war started in Europe, I had yearned for us to have one. The interior light above the front wind-shield of the Plymouth had a corrugated surface on its half-moonshape and from then on, it looked to me exactly like the ammunition belt for a machine gun. I spent hours of imaginary dogfights in the Plymouth, manning the dome light, until after the war, when we could, we traded the Plymouth for a '46 Ford.

The war was wonderful fun. We painted the top halves of our headlights to preserve blackout rules. On our coast, oil slicks from sunken tankers washed up on the beaches. It was thrilling to think that there might be a U-boat looking at you through a periscope right at that moment. We were alert for them whenever we were near the ocean. Coastguardsmen with side arms patrolled our beaches, on the lookout for saboteurs, attracting the attention of young women in bathing suits.

During blackouts, my uncle Paul, the drunk, in his white air raid warden's helmet, was assigned to direct automobiles at a darkened intersection. He usually created a great angry traffic jam. We collected paper for the war, and collected fat in coffee cans. I won a MacArthur medal for collecting so many newspapers. I was years into adulthood before I lost track of it. Most of the ballplayers went to the war. The St. Louis Browns had a one-armed outfielder named Pete Grey.

We studied posters published by Coca-Cola, as I remember, in which the profile of every warplane was presented so that we could spot them at once and know which was ours and which belonged to the Japs or the Krauts. P-40s with the tiger shark nose design that the Flying Tigers used in China. P-41s. P-38s where the cabin was between a double fuselage that stretched back from two engines to twin tails. The unstylish Jap Zeros. The Nazi planes: Messerschmitts, the Stuka dive-bombers with the ugly fixed wheels. The RAF Spitfire. The Navy Corsair. Our planes were always the best-looking. For the first time in my life there were planes overhead often. There were blimps on submarine patrol along the coast, the B-17s and B-24s from Westover Field. The unglamorous transports which one didn't bother to learn the names of. They came low and very loud and everyone would stop and look up. I always hoped it would be an exciting enemy plane, but it never was.

My father was too old to be drafted, but he would receive a commission in the signal corps if he volunteered. My mother put her foot down, as she often did. 'You have a wife and son to take care of' she said while her foot was down. So my father didn't volunteer. The son he had to take care of was aghast and perfectly puzzled. I never blamed him. I blamed my mother.

My cousin Dave was in the Navy in the Pacific. We had his picture on the drop leaf maple table in the living room. Dark blue uniform, white sailor hat on the back of his head, big grin. He had worked out a code with his father to let us know approximately where he was, and when we would go to my uncle John's house he would have Dave's positions marked with colored pins on a big wall map taped up in the kitchen. The names were operatic: Wake Island, Midway, Guam, Tulagi, Guadalcanal, Bougainville, Tarawa, Kwajalein, Truk, Saipan. Jungle and vast blue sea, and tracer bullets in the night and the sound of fighter planes in the sky. My soul spun out across the angry planet like the web from a spider.

Everything was rationed: gasoline, tires, bacon, butter. We used margarine instead. It came lard white with a dye pack included. I used to mix the orange-yellow dye into the recalcitrant margarine until it looked sort of like butter. I never questioned this contribution to the war effort, and felt soldierly doing it. Families with men in the war hung small square flags in the window with a star in the center of the flag, sometimes more than one star. The *star colors told you the status of the warrior. A gold star meant that the warrior was dead, and the Gold Star Mother became one of the enduring icons of my childhood.*

At the movies we saw Bataan, Flying Tigers, Guadalcanal Diary, Thirty Seconds over Tokyo, Wake Island. The Japs were unremittingly wrong. We were brave. Even the misfits learned before the end of the movie that the war had to be won. All of the bomber crews and rifle squads were a melting pot of American ethnicity, Murphy, Martinelli, Shapiro, Swenson and DeLisle. On screen the war was fought by Spencer Tracy and Cary Grant, John Garfield, John Wayne, Robert Mitchum, Humphrey Bogart, Robert Taylor. Of course we would win. Every week at the movies we watched the newsreels which tended to treat the war as an unswerving march by our side toward victory in Europe and the Pacific. No one doubted. There would be no conditions. We required unconditional surrender. Remember Pearl Harbor as we march against the foe... Praise the Lord and pass the ammunition, praise the Lord we ain't a goin' fishing... We're comin' in on a wing and a prayer...

At Mass we said prayers for our boys... Bob Hope went and entertained our boys... The Stage Door Canteen welcomed our boys... The USO brought comfort to our boys. The Red Cross, too... Tokyo Rose urged our boys not to die in vain. How could she do that?

My parents were Republicans and even during the war spoke ill of Roosevelt among their friends. How could they do that? We had some sort of intellectual grasp of the fact that Roosevelt was paralyzed. But it was only that, the knowledge of a meaningless fact, like being aware that calculus exists. Our Roosevelt moved as easily as Churchill. He was never publicly crippled.

There was gasoline rationing and all cars had a sticker designation for how much they could buy a week. We were I think a C sticker. There were ration books. Spike Jones recorded a song called 'Der Fuehrer's Face,' whose lyrics included a forceful Bronx cheer. As the war progressed some of our boys began to return, still jaundiced from tropical fevers, limping from bullet wounds, wearing slings, using canes, deaf in one ear from artillery concussion. They were celebrities, twenty missions over Berlin, veterans of Anzio and Guadalcanal, North Africa and Kwajalein, Italy and France, people who'd fought and killed and seen men die at Iwo Jima and Omaha Beach. They were more important than movie stars or ballplayers. I wished that I could have been one of them. I would have happily suffered what they suffered to have become what they became. If only I was old enough. I never thought about dying in the war. I'd have returned maybe with a wonderful sling, and would shake my head quietly when people asked me about it.

3

His blood count was finally normal. He did a hundred pushups and a hundred situps and a hundred pullups every day. He ran a hard two miles every day. He had lost fifty pounds after he got shot and he appeared to have no muscle at all. But his weight was back up to 190 pounds now. He had done high ironwork before the war and it had given him a lot of muscle density and the density persisted, dormant, until he got well enough to exercise.

By himself, he went to the Paramount Theater and watched *The Best Years of Our Lives* on a Wednesday afternoon. Then he went home and made himself a scotch and seltzer and sat in the chair by the window that looked out onto the street and lit a Lucky Strike and sipped the scotch. He looked at the white package of Luckies. Lucky Strike Green has gone to war. He smiled to himself with no amusement. Didn't we all?

They hadn't lived here long. The furniture had come with the apartment. She had done nothing to personalize it. There were no pictures. He went to the kitchen and made himself a salami sandwich and brought it back in and ate it and drank scotch and looked out the window some more.

There were more cars on the street than when he'd first got out of the hospital and sat staring all day out this window. Gas rationing had ended. There were new models for the first time since the war began. A thick-bodied, black and tan German shepherd dog trotted past the window, alone, going somewhere. Women walked past, some of them good-looking. Burke watched them go. Again, alone in the darkening room, he smiled slightly. For more than a year he had been focused on not dying. Now here he was eating, drinking scotch, smoking a Lucky, looking at girls. He glanced around the small, nondescript, uneventful apartment.

He said aloud, 'I gotta get out of here.'

In the two weeks he spent with her, he remembered, he became adroit. *I can always thank her for that,* he thought. *Marines taught me to shoot. She taught me to fuck.* She had always encouraged him, never criticized, never judged.

'You can talk about anything,' she said, 'my little Mr Marine. You don't have to be tough here.'

When she went to work he would stay at the apartment. She seemed able to set her own schedule at her job, and usually went late in the morning and came home early in the afternoon. He had learned very young to feed himself, and now he bought groceries and made supper. They would eat together in the little kitchen. She would light a candle.

In bed she made him feel heroic. She twisted with pleasure. She cried out with it, calling him 'my dearest boy, my dearest boy.' He had never felt that way before, or since. He'd been tough early, and he'd been brave enough when he had to be; but only in her bed, listening to her gasp with the pleasure of him, had he ever felt heroic. He was a man. He would take care of her, all his life he would take care of her. The memory was harsh. But he couldn't leave it alone. His memory kept going back to it, replaying it, feeling the hot, erotic pain of it. *A fucking man,* he thought. *Mr Fucking Marine Man.*

Three days before his leave was over, in the darkness, enveloped in her heat and smell, he pressed her hard and told her he loved her.

'I know,' she whispered.

'I know,' he said, 'we haven't known each other very long.'

'Time doesn't matter,' she whispered.

'I have to go, day after tomorrow,' he said.

'Shhh.'

'I don't know if I'll come back.'

'You'll come back,' she said.

'Maybe, maybe not,' he said.

'I'll wait for you,' she said.

'Would you marry me before I go?'

It was out. He heard the question linger. A tangible thing, suspended in the dark.

'Of course, little Mr Marine,' she said finally. 'Of course I will.'

4

He packed some clothes and his .45, and took all of the mustering-out money he hadn't spent and walked out of the apartment leaving the door unlocked and the key on the hall table. He had been in the Marines for a while with a guy named Anthony Mastrangelo, whose older brother was a bookie. After he left his apartment he went to see him. They had drinks in the North End in a bar named Spag's.

'You're a strong guy,' Anthony had said. 'How 'bout you be a fighter. My brother Angelo could fix you up with some easy fights.'

'How easy?'

'Easy enough to win,' Anthony had said.

'These guys going in the tank?'

'Sure.'

'And?'

'And we build you a rep,' Anthony said.

'And?'

'And we get you couple big money fights, and maybe me and Angelo bet some side money and...' Anthony made a waffling gesture with his right hand.

They were drinking I.W. Harper on the rocks.

'What makes you think I can do it?'

'In the Corps,' Anthony said, 'I seen you kick the crap out of a couple guys. That big Polack from Scranton, what was his name?'

'Starzinski.'

'And the guy from Birmingham, Alabama?' Anthony said.

'I go in the tank sometimes, too?'

Anthony drank the rest of his whisky and gestured at the bartender. He smiled.

''Course,' he said.

'Okay.'

They hired a trainer and got him ready. He learned quickly,

and after a time no one wanted to spar with him because he seemed not to feel pain, and he came at everyone with a kind of expressionless ferocity that scared even some of the thick-scarred aging Negroes who'd been doing this most of their lives. When they thought he was ready they put him in with a string of palookas. Burke never knew if the fights were fixed or not. It didn't matter. In every fight he went out and attempted to kill his opponent. He won eighteen fights in a row and they began to have trouble getting him matches. Other fighters began to avoid him. Finally they put him in with a tall fighter named Tar Baby Johnson, who had a 35–22 record. For seven rounds Burke went implacably after him, absorbing every punch that Tar Baby threw. He landed very few of his own. Those he did land were mostly on Tar Baby's arms. In the eighth round Tar Baby knocked Burke out with a combination that Burke never saw. Fighters who had beaten Tar Baby Johnson then agreed to fight Burke. Anthony and Angelo dodged them for a while and Burke pulverized several other fighters who fought as Burke did, straight ahead, getting by on toughness. But eventually they had to take another opponent who could box, another rangy black man named Kid Congo, who looked positively delicate opposite Burke's thick white muscularity. Burke was KO'd in the fifth.

'There's fighting,' Anthony said to him, 'and there's boxing. You could beat both these guys up in some alley someplace. You're like a fucking wolverine. But, you got no future in the sweet science.'

Sitting in the reeking cinder block room, holding the ice bag against his face, Burke nodded. It hurt. Burke didn't pay much attention to the fact that it hurt. Most things hurt. Burke was used to it.

'It's our fault,' Anthony said. 'We shouldn't have put you in with the Tar Baby yet. We was supposed to build you up until you got a rep, and then bet heavy and maybe you take a dive for us. But the Tar Baby fucked that up. Make big money on a dive you need to be a heavy favorite, you know?'

Burke shrugged. He got dressed slowly. The scars from Bloody Ridge had faded into insignificant white lines across his belly. His face was swollen. One eye was closed. On the other side of the dressing room, Kid Congo was holding ice against his forearms where Burke's heavy punches had landed. The arms were swollen. He saw Burke looking and grinned.

'You got the heaviest punch I ever seen,' he said.

'I know.'

'But you can't box for shit.'

'I know.'

'He'd kick your ass on the street,' Anthony said to Kid Congo.

'Don't know if he would or not,' Kid Congo said. 'But kicking my ass on the street ain't what this all about.'

Anthony said, 'Watch how you talk, black boy.'

'He's right,' Burke said to Anthony.

Anthony shrugged. Kid Congo slipped into his pink shirt and nodded at Burke and walked out of the dressing room.

'You know my brother Angelo books some bets now and then,' Anthony said.

Burke nodded again.

'He could probably use you to collect some of the proceeds.'

'Okay.'

'Most of the time they'll just give it right up,' Anthony said. 'Even if they don't want to, you'll scare them and they'll do it.'

'And if they don't?'

Anthony shrugged.

'You reason with the fuckers,' he said. 'Money's good. Hours are good. Better than getting knocked on your ass every few weeks by guys like Tar Baby Johnson and this coon. Okay?'

Burke shrugged.

'Okay.'

Bobby

When I was a small boy and we still lived in Springfield my mother would disapprove of my behavior by saying it was as if I lived on Columbus Avenue, which was, in those days, a Negro neighborhood.

I knew that a white fighter named Billy Conn almost beat Joe Louis at the Polo Grounds until he got careless in the thirteenth round. All of us rooted along with the rest of America, or almost the rest, that a white fighter would beat Louis (as long as it wasn't Schmeling). Conn was the closest we got. Lou Nova failed, and Buddy Baer, and Two Ton Tony Galento. I knew that there was a race riot in Detroit in 1943 and President Roosevelt had to send in army troops. I was never clear how it worked in the war, but I was pretty sure Negroes and whites didn't serve in the same units.

I knew that my father would give me a nickel, every Saturday, and I would go up to Wolfe's drugstore on the corner of my street and buy five licorice candies called nigger babies. I knew that the Brazil nuts in the nut mix my mother put out at Christmas were called nigger toes. I knew that there was a high lawn weed, which when it went to seed was called a nigger head. If something was brightly shined my mother would describe it as 'shining like a nigger's heel.' People who spent money foolishly on ostentation were nigger rich.

In my childhood that was what I knew of black people. I had no personal contact. There were none at school. Until we moved to New Bedford, I don't think I ever met a black person. I don't remember my father ever working with a black person. To my knowledge my mother never knew one. Black racism was, thus, a kind of abstraction. One knew it was coarse to call someone a nigger. Impolite. But one didn't worry that they'd move into the neighborhood. It was unthinkable. And no one, in my memory, ever thought about it.

The more immediate threat was Jewish. They could often pass, if one wasn't alert. In 1944 when my father was transferred to

New Bedford they sold their Springfield home to a gentile for $500 less than they had been offered by a Jew. My father had no comment on that. My mother explained that selling to a Jew would betray our neighbors. On the other hand, our family doctor was my father's friend Sam Feldman. I found this unsettling.

In fact, long before I should have, long before I had any information to the contrary, I was suspicious of judgments based on race. I do not know why this was. When we were just barely post-pubescent my friends and I, who had never had sex with anyone, and were years away from doing so, would discuss very seriously whether one of us would have sex with a good-looking Negress. Lena Horne was our most frequent example. I always insisted I would. Some of that insistence was merely an honest appraisal of my feverish hormonality. But there was also a sense that to do otherwise, for racial reasons, would be wrong. Embarrassingly that is, to my memory, my first public position on racial equality. The question of whether Lena Horne would have wanted sex with any of us was never considered.

Later I would read Kingsblood Royal, and watch Home of the Brave and find my suspicions about racial attitudes confirmed. But the suspicions existed prior. Perhaps I simply exemplified a happy quirk of nobility. It would be pretty to think so. On the other hand, years past childhood, as an adult, in psychotherapy, I discovered that I was able to keep my most aggressive impulses in check because I identified with the object of my own aggression. I identified with the victim. Maybe that had something to do with it, too.

5

Few people argued with Burke about payments. They looked into his flat gaze and backed down. If they didn't have money they made arrangements. Angelo liked him.

'Anthony's right,' Angelo said to him. 'You got a nice way with this. You talk to people. They come around.'

'Thanks.'

'You're welcome. I don't want to hurt nobody if it ain't necessary,' Angelo said. 'Guy in the hospital ain't earning money to pay me back. Dead guy is earning even less.'

''Less there's life insurance,' Anthony said.

'Well, 'a course,' Angelo said. 'That's a different story. We get it from the widow, that's excellent.'

'Not a lot of widows going to give Burke any shit,' Anthony said.

'Damn few,' his brother said. 'Generally they cough it up.'

'I don't do widows,' Burke said.

Angelo stared at him.

'Whaddya mean?' Anthony said. 'Why not?'

'I don't feel like it,' Burke said.

Angelo kept looking at him. Nobody said anything for a time.

'You work for me,' Angelo said finally, 'and mostly it matters what I feel like.'

'I heard that,' Burke said.

Angelo looked at Anthony.

'He's your friend,' Angelo said, 'whaddya think?'

'Angelo,' Anthony said, 'it's what you call a hypothetical question, ya know? Burke's done a good job so far. Let's worry about the fucking widows and orphans when it comes up.'

Angelo nodded slowly, staring at Burke.

'Okay,' he said. 'Makes sense, but he got to know that I mean what I say. He don't feel like something that I feel like doing – we're gonna have some trouble.'

Burke made no comment. For all his face showed they could have been talking about Douglas MacArthur.

'Sure,' Anthony said. 'That's fair. Ain't that fair, Burke?'

'That's fair,' Burke said.

'Probably won't come up anyway,' Anthony said. 'You know? Probably not really a problem, anyway.'

'Probably not,' Angelo said.

Neither Burke nor Angelo mentioned the matter again. Later that week Burke got a copy of the final papers ratifying the divorce that he had not contested.

On a Monday evening Angelo took him to dinner. They sat in a dark booth in a place called Mario's, and had spaghetti with marinara sauce, some sliced bread in a basket, and a bottle of Chianti.

'Guy I know,' Angelo said, 'political guy. He needs somebody to watch his back for a while.'

'Because?'

'Because he does,' Angelo said. 'I want to give you to him.'

'What are friends for?' Burke said.

He poured some more Chianti into the short water glass provided and drank some.

'I told him you was tough as a five-cent mutton chop,' Angelo said. 'That you kept your word, and that you didn't have much to say.'

Burke nodded.

'Pay's good,' Angelo said. 'And you step up a level.'

'Guy legit?' Burke said.

' 'Course he ain't legit,' Angelo said. 'He's legit, he don't need his back watched. But he's more legit than I am.'

Burke nodded again. The Chianti was cheap and sour. He drank it anyway.

'You and me are going to have trouble you keep working for me,' Angelo said. 'You know it and I know it. You ain't good at taking orders, and I'm really good at giving them.'

'True,' Burke said.

'Anthony says he owes you from Guadalcanal, and he's my brother.'

Burke didn't say anything.

'You want the job?' Angelo said.

'Sure.'

6

Julius Roach had no visible means of support. He was often consulted by borough presidents. He was often identified in newspapers as a City Hall regular. He sat frequently in the owners' box at Ebbets Field, and the Polo Grounds, and Yankee Stadium. He was photographed with Branch Rickey. Toots Shor knew him, and Walter Winchell. When Mayor O'Dwyer spoke at a banquet, Roach was frequently at the head table, dressed very well.

'My daughter needs looking after,' Roach said to Burke. 'Mr Mastrangelo says you'd be just right for it.'

'Angelo told me it was you,' Burke said.

'I thought it seemly to mislead Mr Mastrangelo,' Roach said. 'Family matter, you know?'

'How old is your daughter?' Burke said.

'Lauren is twenty-five,' Roach said. 'Lovely and accomplished, but foolish in her choice of men.'

'And you want me to help her with the choices?'

Roach was a tall man with too much weight on him and white hair that he wore long and brushed back. His clothes were expensive and cut to make him look slimmer.

'I want you to protect her from the consequences of her choices,' Roach said.

'Such as?'

'Lauren seems to have a proclivity for, ah, violence-prone men,' Roach said.

'Why me?'

'I am a man of some public reputation, and some political prominence, and I want this to be very discreet. The usual sources, private detectives, the police, that sort of thing, would seem to risk public disclosure.'

He always talks like he's addressing a jury, Burke thought.

'What, you think I won't blab?'

'Mr Mastrangelo says you're not a talker. He says you don't care about publicity.'

'Did he say what I do care about?'

Roach smiled. He seemed to purse his lips when he smiled. 'Nothing.'

Burke nodded.

'How do you happen to know the Mastrangelos?' he said.

'Angelo and I have met in the course of our work.'

'I need a gun for this?' Burke said.

'You might. I can get you one.'

'I have one,' Burke said. 'Your daughter want a bodyguard?'

'She hasn't been consulted,' Roach said. 'I have little control over her behavior. But I do control her income. She'll do what she must.'

'Is there a mother?'

'My wife is not at issue here,' Roach said. 'For a man who cares about nothing you ask a lot of questions.'

'I care about whether I want to do something or not,' Burke said.

'Do you want to do this?'

'Why not?' Burke said.

7

Lauren thought he looked like some kind of football player with his thick neck. But she knew he wasn't. He was something else entirely. Though she didn't know what.

'This is Joseph Burke,' her father said.

'And a fine figure of American manhood he is,' Lauren said.

Burke said, 'How do you do?'

'And what do you do, Mr Burke?'

Burke smiled and nodded at her father.

'Ask him,' Burke said.

Lauren looked at her father.

'I've asked Mr Burke to look out for you during this nasty business with Louis.'

'Look out for me?'

'Look out for your safety,' Roach said.

She stared at her father.

'You've hired a fucking bodyguard?' she said.

'Watch your mouth,' Roach said, 'when you speak to me.'

Lauren looked at Burke.

'You mean this… I'm expected to let this, this unwashed thug along everywhere I go?'

'I washed this morning,' Burke said.

'I do mean that,' Roach said.

'And if I say no?'

'As long as you live here and spend my money you'll do as I say.'

Lauren took a cigarette out of a box on the coffee table behind her. She put it in her mouth and looked at Burke. Burke didn't move.

'Do you have a match?' Lauren said.

Burke took a packet of matches from his shirt pocket and offered them to Lauren. She stared at him for a moment and then took the matches peevishly and lit her own cigarette. When she had finished she dropped the matchbook on the coffee table.

'How do you feel about this?' Lauren said to Burke.

Burke picked the matches up and put them in his pocket.

'Fine with me,' Burke said.

'You're prepared to spend every day with me even though I can't stand your presence?'

'I am,' Burke said.

'Doesn't that bother you?'

'Not enough,' Burke said.

'What would bother you enough?'

Burke almost smiled.

'If you paid me more than your father.'

'Oh God,' she said. 'Another flunky. My father buys them by the carton.'

She set her cigarette into a big abalone shell ashtray and let it burn.

'Mr Burke will be here at nine in the morning,' Roach said, 'to take you where you want to go.'

Lauren looked Burke up and down slowly.

'At least,' she said, 'get rid of that suit.'

She turned and walked from the room.

8

Wearing his other suit, a dark blue flannel, with a polka dot tie and a white shirt with a Mr B collar, Burke was outside the Roach apartment on Fifth Avenue at Eighty-first Street when Lauren came out and walked across the sidewalk. The doorman hurried to open the back door. She ignored him and walked around and got in the front seat next to Burke. She had big violet eyes and a wide mouth and honey-colored hair that she wore in a long pageboy. Her clothes cost more than Burke had to his name and she smelled of perfume that Burke knew he couldn't afford. Burke caught a momentary flash of stocking top as she swung her legs into the passenger side and closed her own door. She punched in the lighter on the dashboard. She took a silver cigarette case from her purse and took out a cigarette. When the lighter popped she lit the cigarette. Cigarettes always smelled best, Burke thought, that first moment, with a car lighter. She put the case away, and crossed her legs and shifted a little in the seat so that she could look at Burke.

'Well,' she said, 'you look better, at least.'

'Good.'

'Do you know where the Waldorf Astoria is?' she said.

'Park Avenue,' Burke said. 'Fiftieth Street.'

'I'm impressed,' she said. 'I'd have said you were more the flophouse type.'

'I am,' Burke said. 'I just know where it is.'

At Seventy-sixth Street Burke went east for a block to Park Avenue and turned downtown. He could feel Lauren's gaze.

'Are you carrying a gun?' she said.

'Yes.'

'What kind?'

'Forty-five automatic,' Burke said.

'It's making a bulge in your jacket,' she said.

'Big gun,' Burke said.

'Have you ever shot anyone?' she said.

'Yes.'

He glanced at her. The tip of her tongue appeared briefly on her lower lip.

'Tell me about it,' she said.

'No.'

Her tongue touched her lower lip again.

'You could at least be pleasant,' she said.

'You too,' Burke said.

She opened her mouth, and closed it and looked at him some more. Then she laughed.

'Well,' she said. 'My goodness.'

Burke didn't say anything. Lauren shifted further in the front seat so that she was facing Burke with her legs tucked up under her. She let some smoke out through her nose and watched it dissipate.

'Do you know why you're protecting me?'

'Hundred bucks a week,' Burke said.

'Do you know what you're protecting me from?'

'Whatever shows up,' Burke said.

'And you think you can do that?'

'Yes.'

'Well,' Lauren said, 'if we're to be together, however gruesome that may be, at least we should know each other. Are you married?'

'No.'

'Were you ever?'

'Yes.'

'Were you in the war?'

'Yes.'

'Tell me about all of that,' Lauren said.

'I was in the Marine Corps,' Burke said. 'I got shot. I came home. I got divorced.'

Lauren waited. Burke didn't say anything else. Lauren laughed.

'You should work for *Reader's Digest*,' she said.

Burke didn't say anything.

'Okay,' Lauren said. 'I'll talk.'

Traffic downtown was heavy, mostly cabs. Burke didn't mind the traffic. He wasn't going anywhere.

'I'm a bad girl,' Lauren said.

She looked at Burke. He had no reaction.

'I'm rich and dreadfully spoiled,' she said. 'I spend summers in Bar Harbor and winters in Manhattan. I'm selfish. I'm frivolous. I drink too much and smoke too much and am drawn to the worst kind of men.'

'Like Louis,' Burke said.

'Ah. You do pay attention. Yes. Just like Louis.'

Burke nodded. He cut off a taxi. The taxi blew his horn and held it. Burke paid no attention. Lauren watched him. Again she started to speak, and stopped.

'Louis is like me,' she said. 'And his father's a gangster.'

They stopped at the light at Sixty-first Street. She looked at Burke. Burke was silent, his eyes on the traffic light.

'Frank Boucicault,' she said.

The light turned, Burke let the clutch out and they moved forward.

'I've met him,' Lauren said.

Burke nodded.

'He's very old school, gangsterish. Like the movies,' Lauren said.

'Swell,' Burke said.

'But he has an odd charm about him,' Lauren said. 'Power, I suppose.'

'Probably,' Burke said.

'He's more charming than you are,' she said.

She took out another cigarette and lit it from the dash-board.

'Most people are,' Burke said.

'And Louis is heavenly,' she said.

He could see the tip of her tongue again.

'He's very handsome, tall, slim, dark. He has all his clothes made. He's a wonderful dancer...'

Burke was aware that she was watching him closely. She wet her lower lip again.

'And he's a splendid lover.'

'I'm happy for both of you,' Burke said.

'Does that shock you?'

'That he's a good lover?' Burke said.

'No. Not that. That a girl would say right out that a man was her lover.'

'It doesn't shock me,' Burke said.

The traffic had cleared below Sixtieth Street. Burke made an illegal U-turn at Forty-ninth Street and pulled up in front of the Waldorf. The doorman stepped out and opened Lauren's door.

'Not yet,' she said sharply.

'Excuse me, ma'am,' the doorman said and closed the door.

'Does anything shock you?' Lauren said to Burke.

'Not so far,' Burke said.

'Oh God,' Lauren said.

She opened the car door before the doorman could reach it and got out and walked toward the hotel. Burke got out his side and handed the doorman a five-dollar bill.

'Hold this for us,' Burke said.

The doorman palmed the five as if it had never existed. And Burke went after Lauren into the Waldorf.

9

They were at a very small table in Café Madagascar. Lauren was drinking martinis. Burke had a glass of beer. Lauren was singing along with the band.

'In a quaint caravan there's a lady they call the gypsy...'

A heavy man in an expensive tuxedo came to the table and said hello to Lauren. She didn't introduce Burke.

'Tony Bixley,' Lauren said to Burke when the heavy man left. 'He owns the joint.'

'Friend of your father's?' Burke said.

'He's a friend of both of us,' Lauren said and finished her martini. A cocktail waitress dressed in harem pants brought her another one. Lauren took the olive out and nibbled on it. The band started a new song. Lauren knew the lyrics.

'A rose must remain with the sun and the rain...'

She looked straight at Burke as she sang. Her voice was light but it seemed to be on key. She would probably flirt with a Christmas tree if that was the best available.

'To each his own, I found my own, and my own is you...'

Burke looked around the room. There were palm trees and African masks and murals of African tribesmen hunting lions and tigers. The upholstery of the banquettes along the wall was zebra striped.

'Two lips must insist, on two more to be kissed...'

A languid young man moved among the tables toward them. He was tall and almost willowy, wearing a dark double-breasted suit, a white shirt, and a white tie. His dark hair was long for a man's, and wavy. Burke watched him come. He stopped beside Lauren and said, 'Hello, darling.'

Lauren looked at Burke and then up at the man.

'Go away, Louis,' she said.

'Aren't you going to introduce me to your friend?' Louis said.

'Go away.'

'Oh, but I must meet him, darling. He looks so... so authentic.'

'Oh, for God's sake, Louis,' Lauren said. 'This is Mr Burke. This is Louis Boucicault. All right? Now go away.'

'So,' Louis said. 'My successor. Have you gotten her into bed yet?'

Burke tilted his head back slightly and stared at Louis.

'This can be easy,' he said. 'Or it can be bad. If I have to stand up, I'll put you in the hospital.'

There was enough force in Burke's look to make Louis flinch back a little. Louis knew he'd flinched and two red smudges showed on his cheeks.

'Well,' he said. 'Well, well.'

Burke didn't speak.

'Do you know who I am, Mr Burke?'

'I know who you are,' Burke said. 'I know who your father is. Now take a hike.'

Burke kept looking straight at Louis, his hands resting motionless on the tabletop. Louis hesitated, then he smiled down at Lauren.

'I certainly don't wish to intrude,' he said. 'I'm sure I'll see you again, both of you again.'

Lauren didn't look at Louis. She didn't say anything. Louis bowed slightly toward her and looked at Burke and walked away. He moved very gracefully.

Without a word, Lauren emptied her martini glass, and held it up to the waitress. Then she looked at Burke.

'Wow,' she said.

Burke continued to look at Louis.

'No one has ever talked that way to Louis.'

Louis was at the hat check counter.

'I was hired to talk that way to Louis,' Burke said.

The hat check girl handed a gray felt hat to Louis, and a white silk scarf.

'Everyone is afraid of him,' Lauren said. 'Because of his father.'

Louis draped the scarf around his neck, put the hat on, adjusted it so that the brim raked down over his eyes. Burke watched him as he left. The waitress arrived with Lauren's fresh martini. She looked at Burke's half-empty glass. Burke shook his head. The waitress swished away. Lauren was eating her olive.

'Almost everyone,' Burke said.

'Why aren't you afraid of him?' she said.

'Hard to say.'

42

Lauren held her martini in both hands and looked at him over the top of the glass.

'I love martinis,' she said. 'Do you?'

'No.'

'What do you love?'

'Hard to say.'

Lauren drank some of her martini.

'Well, aren't you funny?' she said. Her voice slurred a little bit. 'You don't fear anything. You don't love anything.'

'Funny,' Burke said.

'I guess I'm a teeny bit funny as well,' Lauren said. 'I… There's something really wrong with Louis. At first you don't see it. He's so charming and good-looking and he has money and clothes and knows his way around and everyone was a little afraid of him. But at first I really went for him.'

'People love funny things,' Burke said.

'Love? My God, you are funny. I didn't say anything about love. I said I went for him. I had hot pants.'

'Maybe you had hot pants for what was wrong with him.'

Lauren sat back a little and put her glass on the table. She looked silently at Burke for a time. Then she picked up her glass and drank and put it down and looked at Burke some more.

'Almost certainly,' she said.

10

The leaves had turned in Central Park, and some of them had fallen. But it was still warm. Burke walked south beside Lauren. She was wearing a long tweed coat, a matching tweed skirt, and a mannish-looking little snap-brim hat that matched the coat and skirt.

'Do you have a cigarette?' she said.

'Camels.'

'I smoke Chesterfields,' she said.

Burke shrugged.

After a couple of steps Lauren said, 'Oh very well, I'll take a Camel.'

Burke took the pack from his shirt pocket and shook one loose. She took it and put it between her lips. He lit it for her. Without taking the cigarette from her mouth, Lauren inhaled deeply, and let the smoke trickle out.

'Why did you get divorced?' Lauren said.

'I was away. She took up with someone else.'

'Away in the war?'

'Yes.'

'Did you like being married?'

'Yes.'

'Do you wish you were again?'

'I don't wish,' Burke said.

Lauren stopped. Burke stopped with her.

'For anything?' she said.

Burke shook his head.

'Good God,' she said.

Burke was silent, his eyes moving as he looked at whoever walked toward them.

'I wish for more,' Lauren said. 'More money, more freedom, more cocktails, more music, more clothes, more canapés, more men. I'm wishing all the time.'

'We differ,' Burke said.

'Don't you get bored? Wanting nothing? Feeling nothing? Isn't it damned dreadfully boring?'

'Life's boring,' Burke said.

They began to walk again toward midtown. Lauren nodded her head as she walked.

'Of course,' she said. 'Of course. That's why you're not afraid of Louis.'

Burke didn't say anything. He was watching two men in dark topcoats as they approached, and passed, and moved away uptown.

'You don't care if you live or die,' Lauren said.

'Not much,' Burke said.

'Is there anything?' Lauren said.

'I'd kind of enjoy shooting my wife's boyfriend between the eyes,' Burke said.

'Do you still love her?' Lauren said.

'No.'

'Then why... ?'

'Better than nothing,' Burke said.

11

Seventh Avenue South, in front of the Village Vanguard, was almost empty when Burke came out of the club with Lauren. There were cars at the curb, and a few taxis cruising, but the late night street, in the warm steady rain, was as empty as any hamlet. Lauren had on a pale green raincoat with a caped top and a belted waist. And a flared skirt. Her matching rain hat had a short bill and was draped in the back like a Foreign Legion cap. Burke carried a black umbrella with a crooked walnut handle.

'Let's walk uptown a ways,' Lauren said. 'I love the rain.'

'Umbrella?' Burke said.

'No.'

Two blocks ahead, in front of a silent Nedick's stand near Greenwich Avenue, a black prewar Cadillac pulled into a no parking area beside a hydrant and Louis got out of the front seat. Burke heard Lauren gasp softly. From the back seat two other men got out. Louis was wearing a trench coat and a Borsolino hat. The other two men wore blue overcoats and scally caps. They were big men. The overcoats were tight. All three men leaned silently on the Cadillac.

'Keep walking,' Burke said.

Lauren put her hand on Burke's arm.

'Don't hold my arm,' Burke said.

Burke's voice was soft, but it was urgent, and Lauren pulled her hand quickly away. Burke shifted the umbrella to his left hand. His pace didn't quicken. He could hear Lauren breathing.

He could hear the click of her heels on the sidewalk. The streetlights were softened by the rain. The colorful lights in the store windows, filtered through the rainfall, had a jewel-like quality. There was no wind. The rain was coming straight down, steady but not hard. A cab rolled by heading uptown, its wipers arching back and forth. They reached the Cadillac and didn't slow. Louis and his escorts didn't speak. Burke looked at them as he walked by, between them and Lauren. Louis smirked at him. There was nothing in Burke's face. They passed Louis. No one spoke. Lauren's breathing was harsh as they walked. Her shoulder touched Burke's. Another cab went past them. They didn't look back. At Fourteenth Street they turned west. Looking back down Seventh Avenue as they crossed the street they could see the Cadillac still sitting there, silent and black in the rain, like some sort of predatory beetle. Louis and the other men were no longer visible. They turned uptown at Eighth Avenue. Both of them looked back. No one was behind them.

At Twenty-third Street, Burke managed to flag a cab and they were in out of the rain.

12

'I don't want to go home,' Lauren said.

Her voice was odd, Burke noticed, more excited than fearful. She sat close to him in the back seat of the cab.

'Where would you like to go?' Burke said.

'The park.'

'Central Park?'

'Yes. I love the park in the rain.'

Burke leaned forward and spoke to the cabbie.

'Ask him if he knows where we can get a bottle of gin,' Lauren said.

The cabbie knew where to get gin, but it would cost them fifty dollars. Burke gave the cabbie fifty dollars. He stopped at a darkened liquor store on Eighth Avenue and went out of sight down an alley to the side and reappeared with a pint bottle of Gilbey's Gin.

They sat under the umbrella, in the light steady rain on one of the rock outcroppings on the west side of the park near Sixty-fourth Street and sipped gin from the bottle. Burke sipped very little.

'Don't you like gin?' she asked.

'I don't,' Burke said.

Sitting in the woods, in the dark, in the rain, he watched for movement in the park. It made him think of Bloody Ridge.

'What do you like?' Lauren said.

'We've been through that,' Burke said.

Lauren drank some gin.

'Do you like me?' Lauren said.

'Sure.'

'I could make you like me a lot,' she said.

Burke didn't comment. Lauren drank some gin. The nighttime park was full of sounds. Squirrels perhaps, night birds. Burke smiled to himself. Rats.

'Louis used to lace gin with ether,' Lauren said. 'It's quite an exotic feeling.'

Burke nodded. None of the park noises sounded human. Lauren drank more gin. She was drunk. But she wasn't sloppy. She was a contained drunk. Almost dignified. She handed him the gin bottle. He didn't drink. She slid away from under the umbrella and stood up suddenly. She was steady enough on her feet. She had risen gracefully. She took her rain hat off and threw it away from her. Burke heard it skitter on the rocks. In the dim light that drifted in from the West Side, Burke could see the rain begin to glisten on her thick hair. She unbuttoned the raincoat and let it slide down her arms into a heap on the rocks behind her. She was looking steadily at Burke. He was pretty sure her eyes had gotten bigger. She unzipped her white dress and pulled it up over her head, and bending forward, slid it down her arms and dropped it on the rock. She wore no slip. Her white underwear had lace trim. She wore stockings and a garter belt. Still looking straight at Burke she smiled and raised her arms over her head and touched the backs of her hands together. The rain slid down her half-naked body. Her thick hair was straightening as it got wetter.

'Shall I go on?' she said.

'Up to you,' Burke said.

If there were ambient sounds in the park, he no longer heard them. He saw nothing moving.

'Would you like to take off the rest?' Lauren said.

Burke's voice sounded a little hoarse to him.

'If you want them off,' Burke said, 'you'll take them off.'

'Yes,' she said. 'I will.'

She slipped out of her underwear and stood naked in the rain except for her garter belt and stockings.

'Do you like garter belts?' she said.

'Sure,' Burke said.

'I love them,' Lauren said. 'They're so… cheap.'

Burke felt himself clench. His breath was quick and shallow. He thought of Bloody Ridge. She stood before him, her arms above her head, her face turned up, the rain making her naked skin slick.

Without looking down she said, 'Would you like to fuck me? Here? On the wet ground? In the rain?'

Burke's throat had narrowed. It was hard to squeeze his voice out past it. He took the .45 out and laid it on the rock close at hand, under the umbrella. He took a deep breath and eased the air out slowly.

Then he said, 'Yes.'

Bobby

I felt very American during the war. I played Paul Robeson's recording of 'Ballad for Americans' often, listening closely so I could remember the lyrics... 'In '76 the sky was red/With thunder rumbling overhead.'

There were soap operas on the radio in the daytime for the women, and adventure serials in the late afternoon so boys could listen to Jack Armstrong and Captain Midnight and Hop Harrigan. I never thought much about it then, but girls probably listened too.

But in the evening we all listened to Jack, Doc, and Reggie on I Love a Mystery. We listened to Jack Benny and Bob Hope and Bing Crosby. We listened to the Shadow. All of us. Children, adults. Once a week, the Lux Radio Theater dramatized popular movies with name actors. Lux presents Hollywood. My memory is that Cecil B. DeMille was the host. He talked in elocution English that had no region. The announcer referred to him as Mr DeMille.

The Fitch Bandwagon... don't despair, use your head, save your hair, use Fitch Shampoo. Duffy's Tavern... Archie the manager speaking, Duffy ain't here. Wistful Vista. Allen's Alley. The Green Hornet and Cato. Steve Wilson and Loreli Kilbourne of the Illustrated Press... freedom of the press is a flaming sword, use it wisely, hold it high, guard it well.

We all shared the same love songs, by the same singers. Crosby and Sinatra. Dinah Shore and Dick Haymes. Bob Eberly. Helen O'Connell. Vera Lynn. The Ink Spots. Jo Stafford.

We all believed in love.

LIFE *magazine appeared every Monday. It was the unifying force of my childhood. Big format. Pictures. Text. LIFE covered everything. Or seemed to. LIFE was there when it happened and it not only told you what happened but explained it, placed it in context. LIFE wrote about sorority parties and medieval princes and labor strikes and Italian peasants and football games in*

Michigan. It covered the war in China between Chiang and the Communists. It covered hearings of the House Un-American Activities Committee. It covered debutante cotillions, managing to get some careful shots of pretty girls getting dressed and making up. It covered the Broadway stage. It had a regular feature called 'LIFE Goes to the Movies' that encapsulated a current feature, telling an abbreviated version of the story in pictures and captions. Life presents Hollywood.

LIFE covered the White House and the Congress and big labor and big business. It covered the New York Philharmonic, and life in small Midwestern towns and the urban renewal of Omaha, and proceedings in the British House of Commons, and exploration of the South Pole, all with the measured certainty of an insider. It had access. It was there. It understood.

And always, at the heart of its coverage, shaping every attitude it espoused and certainly every attitude I learned from it, LIFE offered the vision of a robust and pleasant life lived in a bountiful and beautiful land. A fundamental part of that life was marriage, and the clean and happy sex that went along with it. It was the culminating purpose of any boyhood to marry a fresh and bouncy young white woman with good thighs who bathed often and had a great smile... and settle down and never roam and make the San Fernando Valley my home.

I looked forward to LIFE's arrival each week.

13

They ate breakfast together in Burke's apartment at 3:20 in the afternoon. Lauren's clothes hung drying in the bathroom. She wore one of Burke's dress shirts.

'Your room is very neat,' Lauren said.

'Yes.'

'And all those books.'

'I've had a lot of free time,' Burke said.

Lauren put down her coffee cup and put a cigarette in her mouth. Burke leaned forward and lit it for her.

'Is there anyone you should call,' Burke said, 'tell them you're all right?'

'Daddy is used to me not coming home,' Lauren said.

'And your mother?'

'She doesn't care,' Lauren said. 'Mostly she's drunk.'

Burke lit himself a cigarette. The first one of the day, with coffee, was still a good moment.

'Are we going to talk about last night?' Burke said.

'You one of those guys likes talking about it afterwards?' Lauren said.

'I like to know what the hell went on.'

'I think the term is sexual intercourse,' Lauren said.

'Why?'

'Because you're irresistible?'

'It wasn't about me,' Burke said.

'Why does it have to be about anything?' she said.

'You're not the first woman I slept with,' Burke said. 'But you're the first one I slept with who stripped naked in a public park, and did it on the ground in the rain.'

'Well, aren't we conventional?'

'One minute you can't stand me, the next we're fucking in the rain.'

'Must you be coarse.'

'You like coarse?'

'Oh, you know me so well?'

'Tell me about Louis,' Burke said.

'I have.'

'Tell me more,' he said.

'Do you have any aspirin?' Lauren said.

Burke got her some. She took three tablets and washed them down with coffee.

'Louis,' she said.

She paused and took a deep breath. There were dust motes, Burke noticed, drifting in the light where the afternoon sun shone through the window.

'Louis is what happens when money and power combine with weakness and cruelty.'

'The money and power come from his father,' Burke said.

'Yes.'

She gestured at her cup.

'Pot's on the counter,' Burke said.

'I have a terrible headache,' she said. 'Please be a darling.'

'Of course you have a headache, you drank a pint of gin.'

She closed her eyes and shuddered.

'Please,' she said.

Burke got the coffee and poured her some. Then he sat back down across the table from her and waited.

'Louis likes to cause pain,' Lauren said after a time.

Burke didn't say anything.

'Physical pain,' Lauren said. 'Emotional pain. Psychological pain. It makes him hot.'

'So why'd you go out with him?'

'I… I… guess I like pain,' she said.

'So how come you left him?'

'I guess I don't like it… too.'

'Does he want you back?'

'I don't know. He may get excited just… stalking me.'

'And the guys with him?'

'I'd guess he's afraid of you.'

'Does he like that too?'

'Being afraid of you?'

'Yeah,' Burke said. 'It happens.'

'I don't know.'

'How do you feel about him, now?'

'The same.'

'You like pain and you don't?'

'Yes. I know it's sick. Louis was making me sicker.'

She sniped out her cigarette and took out another. Burke lit it for her. She drank some more coffee.

'I... this is weird. I never told anybody anything like this before.'

Burke leaned back and hunched his shoulders to relax them.

'That's okay,' he said. 'I never heard anything like this before.'

Lauren inhaled deeply and let the smoke out slowly so it drifted in the air in front of her face.

'Maybe last night had something to do with that,' she said.

'Maybe,' Burke said.

14

They were in Harlem at the Plantation. When Herb Jeffries finished singing 'Flamingo,' Lauren leaned across the table and said they were leaving.

'There's always just a mob coming out at the end of the show,' she said as they walked out onto Lenox Avenue. The white bouncer held the door and looked at Lauren's backside as she went by. Burke smiled without showing it.

There are things you can count on, he thought.

They turned uptown and walked to 147th Street where Burke had parked on a hydrant. When he got a ticket, he gave it to Julius and it went away. As they turned onto 147th Street, halfway up the block they could see the black Cadillac, double-parked next to Burke's car. It would have to move before they could get out. Louis Boucicault was leaning on the right front fender of Burke's car, smoking a cigarillo. He had on a black cashmere topcoat with raglan sleeves and a military collar. The coat was unbuttoned. The collar was turned up, and a white silk scarf was draped around it. The same two thugs that they'd seen in the Village were standing near the back of Burke's car. One of them still wore his scally cap. The other man was bareheaded with a crew cut. Both of them wore their overcoats buttoned. Burke heard something that sounded like a tiny squeal from Lauren.

'Stop here for a minute,' Burke said to her.

She stopped and he stepped behind her and, momentarily shielded by her, he took out the big GI .45 and held it in his right hand. Then he stepped out from behind her, putting his right hand against the small of her back.

'Okay,' Burke said. 'Walk.'

He could hear her breathing. The dark old brownstones were blank and unseeing while the alien white people passed. Lauren was making small sounds. At a higher volume she had sounded the same way in the rain. They stopped ten feet from their car, Burke's right arm still around her waist.

'The tough guy and the lady,' Louis said.

With his thumb and the first two fingers, he took the cigarillo out of his mouth and held it in his right hand. There was a full moon, and with the streetlights, it brightened the scene so clearly that Burke could see that Louis's pupils were very small.

'What do you want, Louis?' Lauren said.

She didn't sound frightened but her syllable stress was all wrong, like a bad calypso singer.

'She fucked you yet, Burke?'

Burke neither spoke nor moved.

'Better than you,' Lauren said.

The guy with the crew cut glanced at his partner. They both grinned. Louis looked back and saw them.

'You lying bitch,' Louis said. 'You begged me for more.'

His voice seemed to be pitched higher than Burke remembered. Lauren walked suddenly toward Louis. Burke let the gun hand drop behind the skirts of his topcoat. Lauren slapped Louis across the face with her right hand and then with her left, back and forth. He stepped back against the car and caught his balance. His face was fish-belly white except for the red marks on each cheek where she'd hit him. He made a sort of whining sound, like a dog in pain, then he jammed the lit end of the cigarillo into Lauren's face. She screamed and jumped away, her hands pressed to her face, and doubled over.

'Uh,' she said, 'uh.'

Burke took the .45 from behind his right leg and carefully shot both the bodyguards. The guy with the crew cut first. The shots were like rolling thunder in the dead empty street. Then Burke aimed the gun carefully at Louis Boucicault's left eye and stepped close to him until the gun barrel pressed against the eyeball.

'Put snow on the burn,' Burke said to Lauren.

He patted Louis down, found a pearl-handled .22 derringer in the left pocket of his topcoat, and threw it into the street. Lauren scooped a handful of snow from the plow spill in the gutter. Burke looked thoughtfully at Louis for a moment, the gun still pressing against Louis's left eyeball. No one moved on 147th Street.

'Don't,' Louis said. 'Please. Don't.'

'Shall I kill him?' Burke said to Lauren.

She was crouching beside the car now, holding the dirty snow against her cheek.

'Make him beg,' she said.

'And then kill him?' Burke said.

Lauren didn't answer.

'Please,' Louis said again. 'Don't. Please.'

It was almost as if he were chanting.

'Kill him? Yes or no,' Burke said.

Lauren still didn't speak. Burke suddenly took the gun away from Louis and put it in the pocket of his coat.

'Oh God,' Louis said. 'Oh God, thank you. Thank you.'

Burke hit him with a left hook and knocked him back against the car. Then he hit him with a right hook. And left, and right. The punches were heavy and professional and they came fast. Louis covered his head with his arms and started to cry. Lauren crouched by the car making her little squealy noises again.

Then it was over. Louis had slid down the side of the car to the sidewalk and his head flopped limply against Burke's car. Burke looked at him for a moment and then walked around and looked in the window of the Cadillac on the driver's side. The keys were in the ignition. Burke got in and started the Caddy up and pulled it forward a couple of car lengths. Then he got out, and reached down and took Lauren's arm, got her on her feet, pushed Louis out of the way, and put Lauren in his car and drove her away.

15

They lay naked in bed together in Burke's apartment, smoking, and listening to Martin Block. He lay on his back. Lauren lay on her side looking at the scars across his chest and stomach.

'Are those all bullets?' she said.

'Some is surgery,' Burke said.

'Did it hurt?'

Burke was silent for a time thinking about her question. Lauren rested her left cheek against his right shoulder and looked at him from very close up.

'Would you rather not talk about it?' she said.

'Hurt's not the right word,' Burke said.

'What is?'

'When you first get it, you feel like you've been hit but there's no big pain right away. And if you're lucky the medics get there and fill you full of morphine and it kind of smoothes you out for a while, and then it's like going into a bad tunnel and nothing makes much sense.'

'Were you in the hospital for a long time?'

'Yes.'

'Was that awful?'

'Yes.'

'Do you want to talk about that?'

'The funny thing,' Burke said, 'is I don't mind talking about getting shot. But I mind talking about the hospital.'

Lauren was quiet. The blue cigarette smoke drifted toward the ceiling.

'You killed two men last night,' Lauren said after a while.

'Yes.'

'You were protecting me.'

'Yes.'

'So why didn't you shoot Louis?'

'You didn't want me to.'

'I mean before. Why did you shoot those other men first?'

'They were dangerous.'

'And Louis wasn't?'

'Not like that,' Burke said.

'How does it feel?'

'Doesn't feel like anything,' Burke said.

'Did you like beating up Louis?'

'Seemed like a good idea at the time.'

'Was it like you think shooting your wife's boyfriend would be?'

'Ex-wife,' Burke said.

'Of course,' Lauren said. 'Was that what it felt like?'

Burke didn't answer.

'Was it?' Lauren said.

Again Burke paused.

Then he said, 'No. It wasn't like that.'

On the radio, Buddy Clark was singing 'Linda.' They listened to it. Lauren finished her cigarette and snubbed it carelessly in the ashtray by the bedside, so that it wasn't completely out, and a small acrid twist of smoke rose from it still. Burke leaned across her and put his cigarette out in the ashtray, and then put Lauren's out completely.

'What do you think Louis will do?' Lauren said.

'Hard to say.'

'Do you think he'll try to get even?'

'Maybe,' Burke said. 'Maybe not. Maybe it's the first time anyone ever rubbed his nose in it.'

'Which means?'

'Maybe he's learned something.'

Lauren moistened her lower lip with the tip of her tongue.

'I think he'll try to get even.'

Burke shrugged.

'That's up to him,' Burke said.

'Do you care?' Lauren said.

Burke almost smiled.

'No more than usual,' he said.

'It frightens me,' Lauren said.

'Un huh.'

'And maybe... I don't know... titillates me?'

'Un huh.'

'But you'll be protecting me?'

'Un huh.'

'You won't let him hurt me?'

'No.'

'Or you?'

'No.'

'I care about you.'

Burke didn't say anything. He fumbled another Camel from the pack on the bedside table and lit it and lay on his back smoking.

'I do care about you, you know,' Lauren said.

'Sure,' Burke said.

'I care about myself a little,' Lauren said. 'As long as you're with me, Louis can't get me. Can't get me in any way.'

'Any way?'

'I don't need him,' Lauren said, 'when I'm with you.'

On the radio Martin Block was signing off. Burke inhaled deeply and let the smoke out slowly, watching it rise.

It's make believe ballroom time, the hour of sweet romance.
It's make believe ballroom time, come on children let's dance.

Burke didn't know how much of what he remembered was based on things he'd heard spoken or hinted at, and how much was sheer fantasy which had ripened beneath the ceaseless scrutiny of his imagination. Whatever it was it was detailed and exact.

This boy was Airborne, 101st, Screaming Eagles, wounded at Bastogne. He wore his jump wings, his CIB, his campaign ribbons. His wound had healed, except that he still used a cane to walk.

'Can you dance, Mr Paratroop?' she said.

Bare-legged, blue dress, tiny white polka dots, red high-heeled shoes.

'Sure can,' the boy had said and leaned the cane against a chair. 'Cane's mostly just for meeting girls.'

The band played 'Sentimental journey,' she sang softly to him, '… gonna set my heart at ease…'

'Are you in any pain?' she said softly.

'No. Just a little stiff now, another couple months I'll be fine.'

He was a slim kid, with smooth black hair combed back, and nice even features.

'Where'd you get wounded?' she said, moving her hips against his.

'Bastogne. Last winter.'

'Nuts?' she said.

The boy laughed.

'General McAuliffe? They tell me he said that. I didn't hear him.'

'Was it a bad wound, Mr Paratroop?'

'Depends,' he said, 'what you mean by bad. It hurt like hell. But it got me out of there.'

'Oh God,' she said. 'I'd have been so scared.'

'I was,' he said.

'But you did it.'

'I guess I had to,' he said.

'That's so brave.'

'No braver than anyone else,' he said.

The music changed. 'Kiss me once, and kiss me twice, then kiss me once again…'

'You going home to anyone, Mr Paratroop?'

'Not really,' he said, 'My parents, I guess.'

'No sweetheart?'

'No.'

'Well, maybe, for now, anyway, that will be me,' she said.

When the club closed they walked back to her apartment.

'Do you like scotch?' she said.

'I like pretty much everything,' he said.

She put out Vat 69 and ice and put the soda siphon beside it on the coffee table. He made her a drink and one for himself. She sat on the couch beside him.

'What did you do before the war?' she said.

'I was in college.'

'Did you finish?'

'No. I'll probably go back when I get out.'

She had her legs crossed. Her bare legs were white and smooth. She pressed her thigh against his.

'Have you ever been able to talk about it?' she said.

'The war?'

'Yes.'

'Well, we talk about it some,' he said. 'You know, me and the other boys.'

'But then you have to pretend about it,' she said. 'Have you ever had the chance to really talk about it, all of it, no need for pretense?'

'I guess not.'

'It's hard for men,' she said. 'To talk about feelings.'

She was pressing close to him. He could smell her perfume. He put his arm around her. She put her hand on his thigh.

'Has it been a long time?' she said softly.

She rubbed his thigh gently.

'Long time?' he said.

'Since you've made love.'

He laughed.

'Mademoiselle from Armentiers,' he sang. *'Parlez vous.'*

She laughed too.

'I'll bet there wasn't much conversation,' she said.

'Not much more than *combien*,' he said.

'Have you ever made love with a woman who actually cared about you?' she said.

'Not yet.'

'Well,' she said, 'then it's time.'

She pressed her lips hard against his and opened her mouth.

They were together every night. He was not inept. He'd learned from French professionals. But he insisted that she teach him, and she did show nuance and invention to him. At the most intimate of moments she urged him to let go, to talk about the war, about his wound, about himself.

'Let it all come out,' she said, 'let it go.'

He did his best. He wasn't sure he had that much to say. He told her all the things he could think of.

'Everything,' she would moan, 'everything.'

'Carole,' he would say, 'that is everything.'

She would shake her head and kiss him and whisper that a woman knew. And she knew. There was more. One night he told her he had to report back.

'Did you know I was married?' she said.

'No. Where's your husband?'

'Naval Hospital,' she said. 'He was wounded in Guadalcanal.'

'Marine?'

'Yes.'

'So I guess that means that we'll be saying goodbye to each other,' he said.

'No,' she said.

He looked at her without saying anything.

'I'll go with you,' she said.

'What about your husband?'

'It was a two-week romance, you know, boys going off to war, maybe they won't come back.'

'How bad is he shot up?'

'Bad. They're not sure about him.'

'And you want to divorce him?'

'Yes. I'll divorce him and go with you.'

'I'm not ready to get married,' he said.

'It doesn't matter. I'll go with you. I love my Little Mr Jump.'

'What will you tell your husband?'

'Something,' she said.

Had it happened that way? Burke no longer knew. Fact and anguish had blended so fully and for so long that whatever was factual, this, for Burke, was the truth.

16

Julius Roach sat in the den of his penthouse with Central Park behind him through the picture window. His forearms rested on his thighs. He turned a brandy snifter slowly in his big soft hands.

'I'm not blaming you,' he said to Burke. 'I hired you. You did what you thought needed to be done.'

Sitting opposite, on the leather couch, Burke waited without speaking. He too had a brandy snifter. It sat on the end table next to him.

'And there won't be any police trouble. Frank and I have already seen to that.'

Burke waited.

'But I've known Frank Boucicault for a long time,' Julius said.

He stopped for a moment and sipped his brandy.

'God, that's good,' he said. 'Money can buy you a lot.'

'I hear,' Burke said.

'Frank and I go way back,' Julius said. 'And, damn it, Burke, I can't have some guy working for me shooting up some guys working for Frank.'

'Because?'

'Because business doesn't work that way.'

'Which means?'

'Which means I'm going to have to let you go.'

'Lauren?'

'Frank has promised to control his son.'

'Why didn't he do that a year ago? Save everybody a lot of trouble.'

Julius smiled and swirled his brandy, watching the liquid move in the glass.

'You don't have children, Mr Burke?'

'No.'

Julius nodded.

'Children are difficult, Mr Burke, and it is often easier, except in extremis, to give them their head.'

'But now it's extremis?'

'Yes,' Julius said. 'I will give you two weeks' pay, and I have put in a word for you with a number of people I know who might wish to employ you.'

'Thanks,' Burke said.

Julius stood. Holding the brandy in his left hand, he put out his right.

'There's no animosity,' he said. 'You did a good job, but circumstances…' He shrugged.

Burke didn't stand.

'One more thing,' Burke said.

'Which is?'

'We need Lauren in here to let her know what's going on.'

'I'll inform her,' Julius said.

Burke shook his head.

'She and I need to say goodbye,' he said.

'You may write her a letter,' Julius said.

Burke shook his head.

'I can have you removed,' Julius said.

Burke sat motionless on the couch. His expression didn't change. Julius looked at him for a time.

'But not easily,' Julius said finally.

He went to his desk and picked up the phone and dialed. He spoke into the phone briefly and hung up. In a moment Lauren came into the den. She was smoking a cigarette, and wearing white silk lounging pajamas under a white silk robe.

'The men in my life,' she said and sat on the big leather couch beside Burke and curled her legs under her.

Burke said nothing. Lauren took a drag on her cigarette.

Julius said, 'Mr Burke is leaving us.'

Lauren froze, her forefingers touching her lips, the thoughtless cigarette smoke exhaling gently.

'No,' she said.

Julius nodded yes. Burke said nothing.

'You can't go,' she said to him.

Burke shrugged. Lauren took the cigarette away from her mouth.

'You can't,' she said again, leaning toward him.

Julius said, 'It is not up to him, Lauren.'

Lauren ignored Julius.

'Without you, he'll get me.'

'Frank Boucicault has promised to contain Louis,' Julius said.

'You are the thing I hang onto,' Lauren said. 'You keep me from sliding into the mess.'

'Lauren,' Julius said, 'please, stop the dramatics. I hired Burke when he was needed. I can fire him when he's not needed.'

Still leaning toward Burke, with her eyes fixed on his face, Lauren said, 'I need him.'

'You don't,' Julius said. 'Frank and I have spoken. Louis will not trouble you further.'

'Burke,' Lauren said.

'I don't make the rules,' Burke said.

'Please,' Lauren said.

Burke didn't answer.

'He's a sickness,' Lauren said. 'You're the cure.'

'Enough,' Julius said. 'It is time to bid Mr Burke goodbye.'

For the first time, she looked at her father.

'You miserable prick,' she said. 'You don't care what happens to me.'

'Enough of that language, Lauren,' Julius said.

'Fuck you, enough,' Lauren said. 'Burke's the only stable thing in my whole sick life. Ever. My mother's a drunk, my father's a crook, and all the men I ever meet are degenerates. Don't you dare tell me, *enough*.'

Julius folded his arms across his chest and said nothing. Burke stood suddenly and walked to the window and looked out down at the park.

'I'll go with you,' Lauren said to Burke. 'I'll go where you go, anywhere, just so I'm with you.'

Burke stared out the window, his eyes following a horse-drawn carriage moving slowly uptown through the park.

'You have to take care of me,' Lauren said. 'No one has ever taken care of me… You have to take care of me.'

Burke turned from the window and looked at her silently.

Then he took in some air in a long slow breath and let it out.

'I can't take care of anyone,' Burke said. 'Not the way you mean.'

The muscles in Burke's cheeks twitched. The lines around his mouth were very deep. There was sweat on his forehead.

'There,' Julius said to Lauren. 'Does that satisfy you?'

Lauren's breath was short. It sounded raspy. Her chest rose and fell arrythmically. Tears ran down her face. She kept looking at Burke. He shook his head. She looked at him some more and then her eyes dulled, and her breathing began to regularize. She turned and looked at her father.

'If you think I was corrupt before...' she said.

She stood suddenly and dropped her cigarette on the rug and walked out of the den without looking back. She left the door open behind her. No one moved for a moment. Then Julius came over and picked up the burning cigarette and snubbed it out in an ashtray. He scuffed the burn mark on the carpet with the toe of his shoe, as Burke left.

Bobby

In 1946, five years after the Dodgers lost the 1941 World Series, in the first fully postwar season, in the summer before my fourteenth birthday, in a year when Stan Musial hit .365, the Dodgers and the Cardinals tied for the National League pennant. There was a post-season playoff for the first time in modern baseball history, which for me seemed to stretch back primordially. The pennant was decided in a two-of-three playoff. I felt I was witness to a historical event. The Cardinals won two straight games. Howie Schultz, as I recall, struck out to end the season.

I was heartbroken. But I had puberty to worry about, and, in a few weeks, the pain receded.

In October of that year, Brooklyn Dodgers GM Branch Rickey announced the signing of a Negro player, Jack Roosevelt Robinson, a four-sport star at UCLA, to a minor league contract with the Dodgers' Triple A farm club, the Montreal Royals.

I was thrilled. Once again I was given the chance to bear witness to history. To be around when something happened that people a hundred years from now would write and speak of. I didn't forget the playoff loss to the Cardinals. I haven't forgotten it yet. But this seemed as if it might be sufficient compensation. There were pictures of Jackie and Branch Rickey at the signing. Rickey with his cigar and bow tie. Jackie gleaming black.

By then we had moved to a town east of New Bedford called Mattapoisett where the Dodgers games could still be heard, coming up the coast on WHN, which was now called WMGM. Negroes lived in the town, and went to school with me. I knew them. At least one of them was a friend, which did not please my mother. My mother said that if there was trouble it would be the colored guy that would get blamed and if I was with him, I'd be blamed too. I don't remember now quite what I thought of that position, but I do remember that I continued to be friends with the colored guy in question.

Interestingly enough, in a group that had debated whether to have sex with Lena Horne, no one seemed shaken by Robinson's signing. We were interested and excited, but no more so than we were by, say, the deal that sent Hank Greenberg from Detroit to Pittsburgh three months later. I, being the out-of-place Dodgers fan, was expected to react more intensely than anyone else, and I did. I cannot explain why I was so pleased, any more than I can fully explain why my racial attitudes differed from the norm. I know that I was pleased that the people in the news, doing the historic thing, were the Dodgers.

The war was over... The players were back... The Dodgers were pennant contenders... The team had just done something that no team had done before... I was fourteen... My voice was changing... I hadn't had sex yet... But I would sooner or later... And the uncluttered world lay ahead of me to the horizon.

Hubba, hubba.

17

Mr Rickey was wearing a blue polka dot bow tie and a gray tweed suit that didn't fit him very well. He took some time getting his cigar lit and then looked at Burke over his round black-rimmed glasses.

'Mr Burke,' Rickey said. 'Do you follow baseball?'

'Yes.'

'I'm bringing Jackie Robinson up from Montreal,' Rickey said.

'The other shoe drops,' Burke said.

Mr Rickey smiled.

'I want you to protect him,' he said.

'Okay.'

'Just like that?' Rickey said.

'I assume you'll pay me.'

'Don't you want to know what I'm asking you to protect him from?'

'I assume I know,' Burke said. 'People who might want to kill him for being a Negro. And himself.'

Rickey nodded and turned the cigar slowly without taking it from his mouth.

'Good,' he said. 'Himself was the part I didn't think you'd get.'

Burke didn't say anything.

'Jackie is a man of strong character,' Rickey said. 'One might even say forceful. If this experiment is going to work he has to sit on that. He has to remain calm. Turn the other cheek.'

'And I'll have to see that he does that,' Burke said.

'Yes. And at the same time, see that no one harms him.'

'Am I required to turn the other cheek?'

'You are required to do what is necessary to help Jackie and I and the Brooklyn Dodgers get through the impending storm.'

'Do what I can.'

'My information is that you can do a lot. It's why you're here. You'll stay with him all the time. If anyone asks you, you are simply an assistant to the general manager. If he has to stay in a Negro hotel, you'll have to stay there too.'

'I got through Guadalcanal,' Burke said.

'Yes, I know. How do you feel about a Negro in the major leagues?'

'Doesn't matter to me.'

'Good. I'll introduce you to Jackie.'

He pushed the switch on an intercom, and spoke into it, and a moment later a secretary opened the office door and Robinson came in wearing a gray suit and a black knit tie. He moved as if he were working off a steel spring. He's nobody's high yellow, Burke thought. He's dark black. And did not seem furtive about it. Rickey introduced them.

'Well, you got the build for a bodyguard,' Robinson said.

'You too.'

'But, I ain't guarding your body,' Jackie said.

'Mine's not worth ten grand a year.'

'One thing,' Robinson said, and he looked at Rickey as he spoke. 'I don't need no keeper. You keep people from shooting me, good. And I know I can't be fighting people. You gotta do that for me. But I go where I want to go, and do what I do. And I don't ask you first.'

'As long as you let me die for you,' Burke said.

Something flashed in Robinson's eyes.

'You got a smart mouth,' he said.

'I'm a smart guy.'

Robinson grinned suddenly.

'So how come you taking on this job?'

'Same as you,' Burke said. 'I need the dough.'

Robinson looked at him with his hard stare.

'Well,' Robinson said. 'We'll see.'

Rickey had been sitting quietly. Now he spoke.

'You can't ever let down,' he said. He was looking at Robinson, but Burke knew he was included. 'You're under a microscope. You can't drink. You can't be sexually indiscreet. You can't have opinions about things. You play hard and clean and stay quiet. Can you do it?'

'With a little luck,' Robinson said.

'Luck is the residue of intention,' Rickey said.

He talked pretty good, Burke thought, for a guy who hit .239 lifetime.

Bobby

In April 1947 I was still fourteen. I would be fifteen in the fall. That month Columbia Records brought out Claude Thornhill's 'Snowfall.' RKO released The Bachelor and the Bobby-Soxer, with Cary Grant and Shirley Temple. In South Africa, Zulus danced for the British Royal Family. In China, Communist insurgents withdrew from Yenan in the face of Nationalist advances. Deborah Kerr bought a house in Los Angeles. The Jewish underground burned a Shell oil dump in Haifa. And when the Dodgers played the Braves on Opening Day, Jackie Robinson played first base for Brooklyn.

April 15 was a Tuesday, and my mother let me stay home from school to listen. It was as if I saw the event. Burnished black face. Bright white uniform. Green grass. I remember Red Barber's familiar southern voice saying, I believe, 'Robinson is very definitely brunette.' I remember thinking how marvelously delicate that was. The event couldn't be ignored. But it needed to be reported neutrally. Barber had his own signature way of speaking. A big rally meant that a team was 'tearing up the pea patch.' An outfielder running down a long fly ball was 'on his mule.'

An argument was a 'rhubarb.' If the Dodgers had three men on, the bases were 'F.O.B.' – full of Brooklyns. If a particularly good hitter was coming up in a particularly crucial spot, Barber would give it a proper introduction as in – 'Two on, two out, and here comes Musial.' When he was excited, Barber would say, 'Oh, doctor!' Such language seemed, at the time, the way one was supposed to describe a baseball game. Any other way would be inadequate.

In the newspapers, I read every box score. Not just the Dodgers, but every team. I felt that I ought to keep track of what was going on all over baseball. In Cincinnati, in Washington. I subscribed to The Sporting News and often read the box scores from the high minors. I could name the starting lineup for Montreal, in the International League, and St. Paul in the American Association. You can learn a lot from a box score.

Box Score 1

Brooklyn.	AB.	H.	O.	A.	Boston.	AB.	H.	O.	A.
Stanky, 2b	3	0	0	3	Culler, ss	3	0	0	2
Robinson, 1b	3	0	11	0	Sistl, ss	0	0	0	0
Schultz, 1b	0	0	1	0	Hopp, cf	5	1	2	0
Reiser, cf	2	2	2	0	McCorm'k, rf	4	3	2	0
Walker, rf	3	1	0	0	R. Elliott, 3b	2	1	0	2
Tatum, rf	0	0	0	0	Litwhiler, lf	3	0	1	0
Furillo, rf	0	0	0	0	Rowell, lf	1	0	0	0
Hermanski, lf	4	1	3	0	Torgeson, 1b	4	0	10	1
Edwards, c	2	0	2	0	Masi, c	3	0	4	0
*Rackley	0	0	0	0	Ryan, 2b	4	3	4	7
Bragan, c	1	0	3	0	Sain, p	1	0	0	1
Jorgensen, 3b	3	0	0	4	Cooper, p	0	0	1	0
Reese, ss	3	1	3	2	§Neill	0	0	0	0
Hatten, p	2	1	1	1	Lanfr'coni, p	0	0	0	0
Gregg, p	1	0	1	0	xHolmes	1	0	0	0
Casey, p	0	0	0	0					
†Stevens	1	0	0	0	Totals	31	8	24	13
‡Vaughan	1	0	0	0					
Totals	29	6	27	10					

```
Boston    ..................0 0 0   0 1 2   0 0 0—3
Brooklyn  ................0 0 0   1 0 1   3 0 *—5
```

*Batted for Hatten in sixth. †Ran for Edwards in sixth. ‡Batted for Tatum in seventh. §Batted for Cooper in eighth. x Batted for Culler in eighth. R—Litwhiler, Ryan, Torgeson, Stanky, Robinson, Reiser 3. E—Edwards, Torgeson. RBI—Edwards, Hopp, Ryan 2, Jorgensen, Reiser 2, Hermanski. 2B—Reese, Reiser. DP—Stanky, Reese and Robinson; Culler, Ryan and Torgeson. BB—Hatten 3. Sain 5, Gregg 2. SO—Hatten 2, Sain 1, Gregg 2, Lanfranconi 2, Casey 1, Hits—Sain 6 in 6, Cooper 0 in 1, Hatten 6 in 6, Gregg 2 in 2 1-3. HP—Hatten 1, Sain 1, Gregg 1. WP—Hatten. Winner—Gregg. Loser—Sain. Umpires—Pinelli, Barlick and Gore. Attendance—25,623.

73

18

It didn't take Burke long to pick up the way it was going to be. Pee Wee Reese was supportive. Dixie Walker was not. Everyone else was on the spectrum somewhere between.

In St. Louis the base runner spiked Robinson at first base.

In Chicago he was tagged in the face sliding into second.

In Philly somebody tossed a black cat onto the field.

In Cincinnati he was knocked down three times in one at bat.

In every city he heard the word *nigger* out of the opposition's dugout.

There was nothing Burke could do about it. He sat near the corner of the dugout and did nothing. His work was off the field.

There was hate mail. Death threats were forwarded to the police, but there were too many of them. All Robinson and Burke could do was be ready. After a doubleheader against the Giants, Burke drove Robinson uptown. A gray two-door Ford pulled up beside them at a stoplight and Burke stared at the driver. The light changed and the Ford pulled away.

'I'm starting to look at everybody as if they were dangerous,' Burke said.

Robinson glanced over and smiled. The smile said, *Pal, you have no idea.*

But all he said was, 'Un huh.'

They stopped to eat at a restaurant on 125th Street. When Burke and Robinson entered, everyone stared. At first Burke thought it was Robinson. Then he realized that they were staring at him. He was the only white face in the room.

'Sit in the back,' Burke said to Robinson.

'Have to, with you along,' he said.

As they walked through, the diners recognized Robinson and somebody began to clap. Then everybody clapped. Then they stood and clapped and hooted and whistled.

'Probably wasn't for me,' Burke said.

'Probably not.'

Robinson had a Coke.

'You ever drink booze?' Burke said.

'Not in public,' Robinson said.

'Good.'

Burke looked around. It surprised him that he was uncomfortable being in a room full of colored people. He would have been more uncomfortable without Robinson.

They ordered steak.

'No fried chicken?' Burke said.

'Not in public,' Robinson said.

The room grew suddenly quiet. The silence was so sharp that it made Burke hunch forward so he could reach the gun on his hip. Through the front door came six white men in suits and overcoats and felt hats. There was nothing uneasy about them as they came into the colored place. They swaggered. One of them swaggered like the boss, a little fat guy with his overcoat open over a dark suit. He had on a blue silk tie with a pink flamingo hand painted on it.

'Mr Paglia,' Robinson said. 'He owns the place.'

Without taking off their hats or overcoats, the six men sat at a large round table near the front.

'When Bumpy Johnson was around,' Burke said, 'the Italians stayed downtown.'

'Good for colored people to own the businesses they run,' Robinson said.

A big man sitting next to Paglia stood and walked over to the table. He was big. Bigger than either Robinson or Burke. He was thick-bodied and tall, with very little neck and a lot of chin. His face was clean-shaved and had a moist glisten. His shirt was crisp white. His chesterfield overcoat hung open, and he reeked of strong cologne.

'Mr Paglia wants to buy you a bottle of champagne,' he said to Robinson.

Robinson put a bite of steak in his mouth and chewed it carefully and swallowed and said, 'Tell Mr Paglia, no thank you.'

The big man stared at him for a moment.

'Most people don't say no to Mr Paglia, Rastus.'

Robinson said nothing, but his gaze on the big man was heavy.

'Maybe we can buy Mr Paglia a bottle,' Burke said.

'Mr Paglia don't need nobody buying him a bottle.'

'Well, I guess it's a draw,' Burke said. 'Thanks for stopping by.'

The big guy looked at Burke for a long moment, then swaggered back to his boss. He leaned over and spoke to Paglia, his left hand resting on the back of Paglia's chair. Then he nodded and turned and swaggered back.

'On your feet, boy,' he said to Robinson.

'I'm eating my dinner,' Robinson said.

The big man took hold of Robinson's arm, and Robinson came out of the chair as if he'd been ejected and hit the big guy with a good right hand. Robinson was nearly two hundred pounds, in good condition, and he knew how to punch. It should have put the big man down. But it didn't. He took a couple of backward steps and steadied himself and shook his head as if there were flies. At Paglia's table everyone turned to look. The only sound in the room was the faint clatter of dishes from the kitchen. Burke stood.

'Not up here,' Robinson said. 'I'll take it downtown, but not up here.'

The big man had his head cleared. He looked at the table where Paglia sat.

'Go ahead, Allie,' Paglia said. 'Show the nigger something.'

The big man lunged toward Robinson. Burke stepped between them. The big man would have run over him if Burke hadn't hit him with a pair of brass knuckles. It stopped him but it didn't put him down. To do that Burke had to get a knee into his groin and hit him again with the brass knuckles. The big man grunted and went down slowly, first to his knees, then slowly toppling face forward onto the floor.

There was no sound in the room. Even the kitchen noise had stopped. Burke could hear someone's breath rasping in and out. He'd heard it before. It was his.

The four men at Paglia's table were on their feet. All of them had guns. Paglia remained seated. He looked mildly amused.

'Don't shoot them in here,' he said. 'Take them out.'

Burke's .45 was still on his hip. A thin tall man with high shoulders said, 'Outside,' and gestured with the .38 belly gun he carried. He held the weapon like it was precious.

'No,' Robinson said.

'How about you, pal?' the gunman said to Burke.

Burke shook his head. The gunman looked at Paglia.

Paglia said, 'Okay, shoot them here. Make sure the niggers clean up afterwards.'

The gunman smiled. Burke could see that he liked the work.

'Which one of you wants it first?' he said.

At the next table a small Negro with a thin mustache, wearing a cerulean blue suit, said, 'No.'

The gunman glanced at him.

'You too, boy?' he said.

At the table on the other side of them a large woman in a too-tight yellow dress said, 'No.' And stood up.

The gunman glanced at her. The small Negro with the mustache stood too. Then everyone at his table stood. The woman in the too-tight dress moved in front of Robinson and Burke. The people from her table joined her. The people from Mustache's table joined them. Then everyone in the room was on their feet, making an implacable black wall between Robinson and the gunman. Burke took his gun out. Robinson stood motionless, balanced on the balls of his feet. From the bar along the far side of the room came the sound of someone working the action of a pump shotgun. It was a sound, Burke thought, like the sound of a tank, that didn't sound like anything else. The round-faced bartender leaned his elbows on the bar aiming a shotgun with most of the stock cut off.

The gunman looked at Paglia again. They were an island of pallid faces in a sea of dark faces. Paglia got to his feet for the first time. His face was no longer amused. He looked at Burke through the crowd, and at Robinson, and seemed to study them for a moment.

'His name I know,' Paglia said, jerking his head toward Robinson. Then he stared hard at Burke as if committing him to memory. 'What's your name?'

'Burke.'

Paglia nodded thoughtfully. Looking at Burke through the crowd of black faces, his eyes seemed to refocus, as if recalling something.

'Burke,' he said.

The room was quiet.

'Burke.'

He nodded again and kept nodding. Then he jerked a thumb toward the big man, who had managed to sit up on the floor among the forest of Negro feet. Two of the other men with Paglia eased through the crowd and got the big man on his feet. They looked at Paglia. Paglia looked at Burke again, then turned without speaking and walked out. The gunman put his belly gun away, sadly, and turned and followed Paglia. The other men, two of them helping the big guy, went out after him.

The room remained still and motionless. Then Robinson said again, 'Not up here,' and everyone in the room heard him and everyone in the room began to cheer.

'Lucky thing this is a baseball crowd,' Burke said to Robinson.

Robinson looked at Burke for a moment as if he were somewhere else. Then he seemed slowly to come back. He smiled.

'Yeah,' he said. 'You scared?'

'No.'

'Why not?'

Burke shrugged.

'No,' Robinson said. 'I want to know. You could have run off. You didn't. Aren't you scared of getting killed?'

'Don't much care,' Burke said.

'About dying?'

'About anything,' Burke said.

19

'You are not here to take his side,' Mr Rickey said. 'If someone throws a rotten egg at him you let it go. If someone calls him a vile jigaboo you pay no attention. If Robinson comes into the stands after the miscreant who threw the egg, you stop him. If someone tries to shoot Robinson, you stop him. Do you understand?'

'I do.'

Burke was behind the visitors' dugout at Wrigley Field, looking around the stands. The game was peripheral, but he knew that Robinson was two for two off a struggling Claude Passeau, and the Dodgers had a six-run lead in the fifth inning. Most of the cheap seats were filled with black faces. The box seats, where Burke was, were half empty. A tall thin guy with high shoulders sat down in the seat beside Burke.

'How ya doing?' he said.

He had a bag of peanuts.

'Fine,' Burke said.

'Remember me?' he said. 'The shine joint up on Lenox Ave.'

'I do,' Burke said.

'I got a message,' he said.

Burke didn't say anything. The thin high-shouldered man took a peanut from his bag, and shelled it. Both men were staring at the field. But Burke's full concentration was on the thin man.

There was movement on the field. Somebody had hit the ball. Somebody had caught it.

'For me?' Burke said.

'For you and young Rastus.' The thin guy nodded toward the field.

Burke didn't say anything. The inning must have ended. Teams were coming in and going out. The thin man ate another peanut.

'Mr Paglia says that you and the nigger going to die this season.'

'Why tell me about it?' Burke said. 'I'll know when it happens.'

The thin guy grinned.

'Don't rattle too easy, do you?'

'I don't,' Burke said.

'Me either. Mr Paglia's insulted. So he wants you to know ahead of time. He wants you to know it was him when it happens. He wants you to sweat about it for a while.'

'Who's going to do the shooting?'

'Probably be me,' the thin guy said.

Burke nodded. Beer was being passed. Peanuts were tossed. The base paths were reddish. The grass was bright green. Behind the left field fence, across the street, people were watching the game from the roof of a building.

'I'll keep it in mind,' Burke said.

The thin man ate his peanuts. He was careful about it. Open the shell, take out the nuts inside, throw away the shells, pop the nuts into his mouth, chew slowly, his eyes on the field.

'Still got that big forty-five?' he said after a while.

'Yep.'

He ate three more peanuts. They smelled good.

'Kind of clumsy to pull,' he said.

'Knock you on your ass, though.'

'True.'

He offered his bag of peanuts. Burke took a couple. The game on the field seemed silent and remote.

'Lemme ask you something,' the thin guy said.

Burke didn't say anything.

'I seen you,' he said. 'Up in Harlem. You can handle yourself. Fists. Gun. You know what you're doing.'

Burke ate his peanuts.

'So how come,' the thin guy said, 'you're hanging around with this buck nigger like he was your cousin?'

'Can't sing or dance,' Burke said.

'It's work,' the thin man said.

Burke nodded.

'There's a lot of work,' the thin man said.

'Like walking behind a fat thug who can't do his own shooting?'

'He don't have to no more,' the thin man said.

'You do it.'

The thin man grinned.

'Can't sing or dance,' he said.

The ex cathedra voice of the PA announcer said that Stan Hack was batting for Claude Passeau. Hack.

'So how come?' the thin man said.

'It's a good payday,' Burke said.

'You a nigger lover?'

'I don't love much of anything,' Burke said.

The thin man nodded as if he knew about that.

'You willing to die for this coon?' he said.

'Been willing to die for a lot less,' Burke said.

The thin guy was quiet for a while. Then he shrugged.

'Well,' he said. 'You signed on for it.'

Hack popped the ball high and foul to the left side. They watched Spider Jorgenson catch it in the third-base coaches' box and the inning was over. When Burke looked back, the thin man was gone.

Box Score 2

Chicago.	AB.	H.	O.	A.	Brooklyn.	AB.	H.	O.	A.
Lowrey, 3b-lf	5	1	4	2	Stanky, 2b	4	2	3	2
Rickert, lf	2	0	1	0	Robinson, 1b	3	0	9	1
Schenz, 3b	0	0	0	0	Reiser, cf	2	0	3	0
§Frey	1	0	0	0	Walker, rf	4	2	1	0
Pafko, cf	5	3	3	0	Hermanski, lf	2	1	2	0
Cavarretta, 1b	5	2	5	1	Furillo, lf	2	1	2	0
Scheffing, c	3	0	1	1	Edwards, c	5	2	4	0
†Dallessandro	1	0	0	0	Jorgensen, 3b	4	2	1	0
Erickson, p	0	0	1	1	Reese, ss	2	0	1	5
Nicholson, rf	2	0	1	0	Hatten, p	3	1	1	0
Johnson, 2b	3	1	4	3	Casey, p	0	0	0	0
Merullo, ss	3	0	4	2		—	—	—	—
Wyse, p	1	0	0	3	Totals	31	11	27	8
*McCullough	1	0	0	0					
Meers, p	0	0	0	1					
‡Livingston, c	2	1	0	0					
	—	—	—	—					
Totals	34	8	24	14					

```
Chicago  ................... 0 0 0   0 0 0   0 2 4— 6
Brooklyn  ................. 0 0 1   0 2 0   0 7 *—10
```

*Batted for Wyse in sixth. †Batted for Scheffing in eighth. ‡Batted for Meers in eighth. §Batted for Schenz in ninth. R—Lowrey, Schenz, Nicholson, Merullo, Livingston 2, Stanky 2, Robinson 2, Reiser, Walker, Furillo, Jorgensen 2, Reese. E—Walker, Merullo, Lowrey, Reese, RBI—Hatten, Reiser, Walker 4, Cavarretta 2, Stanky 2, Furillo 2, Lowrey 3. 2B—Jorgensen 2, Johnson, Livingston, Cavarretta, Stanky, Walker HR—Furillo, Lowrey. DP—Stanky and Reese; Wyse, Merullo and Cavarretta; Reese, Stanky and Robinson 2; Lowrey, Johnson and Cavarretta. BB—Wyse 4, Meers 3, Erickson 2, Hatten 4, Casey 2. SO—Meers 1, Hatten 4. Hits—Wyse 6 in 5, Meers 0 in 2, Hatten 6 in 7 2-3. HP—Wyse 1, Erickson 1. Winner—Hatten. Loser—Wyse. Umpires—Barlick, Gore and Pinelli. Attendance—18,030.

Bobby

I played first base on the junior high school team and hit .303 that year, though the averages were sometimes suspect because the fifth-grade teacher was our scorekeeper and she gave everyone a hit who reached base. No one ever reached on an error. The school supplied the uniforms, grayish woolens with blue numbers. They had to be worn by a new player after you left, so they were of a generic size, and tended to bag. The school also issued the catcher's mitt and the first baseman's mitt. It was a claw, a three-fingered glove with the fingers laced together.

While I listened to the Dodgers games, I usually kept a scorecard, and, when my father came home from work, I would share it with him. It never occurred to me that he would be less interested than I, and, in fact, if he was, he never said.

If I missed a game, I could listen, usually with my father on the screened front porch, at seven in the evening, to a fifteen-minute recreation of the game, complete with sound effects and an announcer, it might have been Ward Wilson, simulating play by play. If I hadn't listened to the real game I tried not to know the score when I listened to the re-creation. If the Dodgers had lost, and I knew it, I didn't listen. The knowledge was painful enough without having it dramatized.

Other things were taking place in the world. I knew that there was a civil war in China, something with the Communists. I knew there was something going on in Greece. I knew Truman was president and George Marshall was secretary of state. I now knew the facts of life. I knew that it was thought dangerous to swim in the summer because you might get infantile paralysis. I knew a lot. But I didn't care. What I cared about was sex and the Brooklyn Dodgers.

20

There was no other white person in sight when Robinson and Burke got out of the cab in St. Louis. The Royal Crest Hotel was a narrow three-story building with dingy red asphalt shingle siding and dirty windows. There was no doorman. The door was narrow and had a dirty glass panel. It opened into a pinched lobby, lit by a hanging bulb, with just room for a small reception desk behind a wire mesh partition. The place smelled bad. The desk man was a thick-bodied Negro with yellowish skin and a fat neck. He looked at them without speaking.

'I called earlier,' Burke said. 'About a room, for me and Mr Robinson.'

The desk man's eyes shifted.

'Didn't tell me you was white,' the desk man said.

'Forgot,' Burke said. 'We need a double room.'

'Colored only,' the desk man said.

'I'm with him,' Burke said. 'Pretend I'm a mulatto.'

The desk man stared past them at the front door.

'Colored only,' he said.

Robinson took a five-dollar bill from his pocket and laid it on the counter in front of the little opening in the wire mesh.

'We need the room,' he said.

The desk man stared at it.

'Ain't even sure that it ain't against the law to domicile colored and white together,' he said.

A set of narrow stairs wound behind the reception desk. A colored man and woman came down the steps and saw Burke and stopped abruptly and stared at him. Then they quickly looked away, skirted him as widely as the small space permitted, and slipped out the front door.

Burke took the .45 from under his coat and aimed it carefully at the desk man's nose.

'What's the law on me shooting you in the fucking nose?' Burke said.

The desk man shrank back a little before he froze still. Robinson put his hand on Burke's arm and pushed the gun down.

'Step outside a minute,' he said. 'Let me talk to this man.'

Burke put the gun away and went and stood outside the front door and looked at the street. It was hot, the way Guadalcanal had been, steaming and dense. The buildings came right to the sidewalk. Around their foundations weeds grew. Where there was paint it was faded and peeling. Four or five small black children in shabby clothes stood across the street from the hotel and stared at Burke. A window went up in the paintless gray building behind them and a woman's voice shouted something Burke couldn't hear. The kids turned and straggled away down the littered alley between the houses. A blue 1939 Plymouth sedan went by. It slowed as it drove past Burke. Dark faces stared out of its windows at him. An empty pint bottle was tossed out the window. The bottle broke and the car picked up speed and drove away. The door behind Burke opened.

'Desk clerk decided to let us in,' Robinson said.

They went in. The desk clerk wouldn't look at Burke. They walked up the stairs behind the desk, two flights, to a room that looked out at the sagging porch on the back of a tenement. The stairs smelled as if someone had vomited. When Robinson opened the door, the heat came out like a physical thing. Robinson walked to the one window and pushed up. The window was stuck. He put a hand on each corner and spread his legs and bent his knees and heaved. The window didn't budge. He looked at Burke.

'Take one side,' he said.

Burke stood on the left side and Robinson on the right.

'On three,' Robinson said.

He counted. At three they heaved, and the window went up. They looked at each other for a moment, and Robinson nodded very slightly. Each of them almost smiled. The air outside wasn't much better.

Box Score 3

Brooklyn.	AB.	H.	O.	A.	St. Louis.	AB.	H.	O.	A.
Stanky, 2b	3	2	2	2	Schoend'st, 2b	4	2	3	4
Gionfriddo, rf	2	0	1	1	Moore, cf	6	2	2	0
Robinson, 1b	5	2	6	0	Musial, 1b	3	2	10	1
Furillo, lf	4	1	3	0	Kurowski, 3b	5	1	0	1
Snider, cf	4	1	2	0	Slaughter, lf	4	2	1	0
Reese, ss	3	1	4	2	Dusak, lf	1	0	1	0
Jorgensen, 2b	4	0	1	3	Medwick, rf	3	2	0	0
Bragan, c	4	0	5	1	Northey, rf	1	0	1	0
Hatten, p	2	0	0	0	Marion, ss	4	3	1	1
Gregg, p	1	0	0	1	Rice, c	5	2	6	2
*Miksis	1	0	0	0	Pollet, p	5	1	2	3
Totals	33	7	24	10	Totals	41	17	27	12

Brooklyn	0 0 0	0 0 0	0 3 0— 3
St. Louis	0 2 1	0 2 2	3 1 *—11

*Batted for Gregg in ninth. R—Stanky, Robinson. Furillo, Schoendienst, Moore, Musial 2, Medwick 2. Rice, Marion 3. Slaughter. E—Reese, Moore. RBI—Moore 3. Pollet 2. Rice, Marion 2. Kurowski 2, Furillo, Snider, Reese, Schoendienst. 2B—Rice, Moore, Marion, Kurowski, Stanky. RB—Hatten 2, Pollet 6, Gregg 2. SO—Hatten 2, Pollet 6, Gregg 2. Hits—Hatten 10 in 5. HP—Hatten 2. Loser—Hatten. Umpires—Gore, Pinelli and Barlick. Attendance—29,686.

21

After a night game at Crosley Field it took them a long time to find a cab. The white cabbies wouldn't pick up a Negro, and the black cabbies were afraid to pick up a white man. Finally Burke went and stood in the doorway and Robinson flagged a cab driven by an aging gray-haired black man. Robinson got in.

'Looking for a place to eat, open late,' Robinson said.

'Sho', the cabbie said. 'Take you over to Gaiter's. Nice southern cookin'.'

'Good,' Robinson said.

He gestured at Burke.

'Wait till my friend gets in,' Robinson said as Burke stepped out of the doorway and walked across the sidewalk.

'Jesus Christ,' the cabbie said.

'It's okay,' Robinson said. 'You know who I am?'

'I do,' the cabbie said. 'But I can't take no white man.'

'He can slouch way down,' Robinson said.

'I get lynched carrying some ofay,' the cabbie said. 'You want me gettin' lynched?'

Burke got into the car and sat beside Robinson in the back seat.

'We can't eat together anywhere that's open now, less we go to the right part of town,' Robinson said. 'We need to eat.'

Burke took out a twenty-dollar bill, folded it in half the long way, and held it toward the cabbie. The cabbie eyed it. He ran the tip of his tongue over his lower lip. Then he took the bill, folded it again and tucked it into his shirt pocket.

'White gennelman has to sit way down and back,' the cabbie said to Robinson.

He didn't look at Burke.

Robinson said, 'Thank you,' and the cab pulled away from the curb. The cabbie drove with both hands on the wheel, careful at cross streets, slowing at intersections. He let them off on a near empty street in front of a glass-fronted restaurant with a large Schlitz beer sign glowing in the window. The door was canopied in purple canvas and on the canvas in gold letters was GAITER'S FINE DINING.

'I can't be waiting for you,' the cabbie said.

'Free country,' Burke said.

Robinson and the cabbie looked at each other for a moment. Burke caught the look.

'Sort of,' Burke said.

The cab pulled away as soon as they were out. They went into the restaurant. It was smoky, crowded and noisy, with a lot of colored lights and a piano player near the bar. When Burke came in there was a pause in the hubbub. Burke had heard it before. The customers began to talk again as Burke and Robinson stood waiting to be seated. A balding Negro in a tuxedo, carrying menus under his arm, stared at Burke for a moment, then looked at Robinson, and, after another moment, back at Burke.

Then he said, 'This way please,' and led them toward a table in the back. As they moved through the restaurant the piano player began to play 'White Christmas.' Four young men sitting together nearby glared at Burke. There was challenge in the glare. Burke ignored them.

'The "White Christmas" business was for you,' Robinson said.

'I sort of guessed that,' Burke said.

'Young bucks over there,' Robinson nodded toward them, 'might work themselves up enough to make some trouble.'

Burke shrugged and picked up his menu.

'What's good here?' he said.

'You think I know the food in every Negro restaurant in America?' Robinson said.

'Figured there might be some sort of natural rhythm to it,' Burke said.

Robinson nodded. For a moment his blue-black face relaxed into a short smile.

'I'm going to have the meat loaf,' Robinson said. 'Side of macaroni and cheese.'

'Sounds good,' Burke said.

While they waited for their food, Burke had a Vat 69 on the rocks. Robinson had a Coke. The four young men at the far table continued to drink Four Roses and ginger ale, and look at Burke.

'This the way it always is?' Burke said.

'Is what the way it always is?' Robinson said.

'Trouble getting a cab, trouble finding a place to eat, trouble getting a hotel room?'

'That's the way it always is,' Robinson said.

'Makes everything hard,' Burke said.

'You learnin',' Robinson said.

His voice seemed to darken into a Negro sound as he talked.

'Got to be careful,' Robinson said. ' 'Bout everything. Be careful who you look at, who you talk to, what you say, where you sit, where you walk, where you live, where you travel. Can't depend on cops. Finding a bathroom is a problem. Buying cigarettes. Riding in an elevator. Getting a drink of water.'

One of the black men at the table near them called over to Burke, 'Hey, white boy.'

Burke turned and looked at him without expression. He was a tall man with yellow-brown skin and longish hair combed straight back and glistening with pomade.

'That's right, Sow Belly, I talking to you.'

Still looking at the pomaded Negro, Burke said to Robinson, 'If there's trouble we leave.'

Robinson said, 'I know.'

The Negro man continued.

'Who that you with? You with your house nigger? You think that make it all right?'

Burke's hands rested motionless on the table. His face was blank. The Negro stood suddenly and walked to the table.

'You talk?' he said. 'Or you too good to talk with a nigger?'

'Don't make a mistake,' Burke said to him softly.

'Mistake,' the man said. 'Shit.'

He paused suddenly and looked at Robinson again.

Robinson nodded his head at him.

'You...' the man said.

Robinson nodded again. At the other table the man's three companions were staring now at Robinson.

'Mutha fuck,' the man said.

He looked at Burke.

'You with him?' he said.

'I am,' Burke said.

The man looked at Robinson.

'Sorry,' he said. 'I didn't know.'

Robinson smiled.

'Ah'm sorry to have bothered you,' the man said.

'It's all right,' Robinson said. 'Enjoy your dinner.'

'Yes. You bet. I... Good luck, Jackie.'

'Thank you.'

The man went back to his table. Everyone in the room turned and looked at Robinson. In a moment a waitress brought their food.

'Everybody in the room now knows who you are,' Burke said as he ate.

'Yes.'

'That bother you?' Burke said.

'Yes.'

After dinner Burke and Robinson stood on the garish street. A brindled dog with one ear down limped past them. Several cabs passed them without slowing.

'All the cabbies are Negro,' Robinson said, 'in this part of town. They won't pick us up because of you.'

'And if we walk ten or twelve blocks to a white neighborhood?' Burke said.

'The white cabbies won't pick us up because of me.'

They stood silently for a moment watching the yellow dog disappear into an alley.

'How far you figure it is to walk to the hotel?' Burke said.

''Bout an hour and a half,' Robinson said. ' 'Course you got to carry that big forty-five.'

'I've walked further than that,' Burke said, 'carrying more.'

'Enlisted?' Robinson said, as they headed downtown under the disinterested streetlights.

'Yeah,' Burke said. 'You?'

'Commissioned.'

'You want to call cadence?' Burke said.

'You start,' Robinson said.

In the uncertain light, on the exhausted street, he might have been smiling.

Jody was there when you left.
You're right.
Your baby was there when you left.
You're right.
But you ain't there 'cause you left.
You're right...

Box Score 4

Brooklyn.	AB.	H.	O.	A.	Cincinnati.	AB.	H.	O.	A.
Stanky, 2b	5	0	4	0	Baumh'tz, rf	4	1	1	0
Robinson, 1b	4	1	3	0	Tatum, cf	5	1	2	0
Reiser, cf	2	2	3	0	Hatton, 3b	3	0	0	2
Miksis, 3b	0	0	0	0	Haas, 1b	3	3	12	0
§Vaughan	1	1	0	0	Mueller, c	4	0	3	0
Walker, rf	4	0	3	0	Lukon, lf	4	0	4	0
Furillo, lf-cf	5	2	1	0	Vollmer, lf	0	0	0	0
Edwards, c	5	3	9	1	Miller, ss	1	0	2	3
Rojek, 3b	3	1	0	2	Adams, 2b	3	1	3	7
Hermanski, lf	1	0	0	0	V'der M'r, p	1	0	0	2
Reese, ss	3	2	1	3	Beggs, p	2	0	0	0
Taylor, p	1	0	0	0	Shoun, p	0	0	0	0
Melton, p	0	0	0	0	Gumbert, p	0	0	0	0
King, p	0	0	0	0					
*Bragan	1	0	0	0	Totals	30	6	27	14
Gregg, p	0	0	0	1					
†Lavagetto	1	0	0	0					
Chandler, p	0	0	0	0					
Barney, p	0	0	0	0					
‡Snider	1	1	0	0					
Totals	37	13	24	7					

```
Brooklyn ................0 1 0   1 0 0   0 0 3—5
Cincinnati .............0 0 4   0 0 0   3 0 *—7
```

*Batted for King in fourth. †Batted for Gregg in sixth. ‡Batted for Barney in ninth. §Batted for Miksis in ninth. R—Robinson, Furillo, Edwards, Reese, Snider, Baumholtz, Tatum, Miller 2. Adams, Vander Meer, Beggs. E—Edwards 2, Chandler. RBI —Tatum 2, Haas 2, Baumholtz, Hatton, Reese 2, Furillo, Robinson, Stanky. 2B—Reiser, Reese, Snider. SB—Miller. DP—Miller, Adams and Haas; Adams and Haas; Adams, Miller and Hass. BB— Taylor 3. Melton 2. Chandler 1. Barney 3. Vander Meer 5. SO—Gregg 2, Barney 6, Vander Meer 2, Gumbert 1. Hits—Taylor 0 in 2 (none out in third). Melton 0 in 1-3. King 1 in 2-3. Gregg 0 in 2. Chandler 3 in 1 (none out in seventh). Vander Meer 0 in 6. Beggs 0 in 2 1-3. Shoun 1 in 1-3. Winner—Vander Meer. Loser—Taylor. Umpires—Barlick, Gore and Pinelli. Attendance—27,164.

22

In Boston to play the Braves, Robinson was able to stay at the Hotel Kenmore with the rest of the team. Burke stayed with him. There was a night game Friday and when they got back to the hotel, someone had slipped a letter under the door addressed to Jackie Robinson. Robinson opened it and read it, holding the envelope in his left hand, and the letter in his right, his dark eyes moving without expression over the page. When he got through he read it again. After the second reading, he handed the letter to Burke. It was handwritten in lavender ink, in a carefully rounded Palmer method hand.

Dear Jackie,

I hope you don't mind if I call you Jackie, but Mr Robinson sounds so odd for a Negro. Don't get me wrong, I am crazy about you. I will see you play tonight at the game, and I'm going to see you play tomorrow afternoon. I love to watch you. I have tickets to all the Dodger games in Boston this year. I'm dying to meet you. It's a day game tomorrow and maybe afterwards I could come to your room and introduce myself. I just know you'd be so gorgeous close up. You can call me at C07-3965. I look forward to hearing from you. I've enclosed a recent photograph of myself.

Affectionately,

It was signed Millicent, and both i's were dotted with a circle.

'Picture?' Burke said.

Robinson took a black-and-white snapshot out of the envelope and looked at it and handed it to Burke. It was a big-breasted blond woman in a one-piece bathing suit, standing on her toes at the beach, with her chin tilted up and both hands behind her head.

'White,' Burke said.

'Blond white,' Robinson said.

Burke put the picture down on the bureau and sat on one of the twin beds. Robinson stood at the window, looking out at the air shaft. Burke swung his feet up on the bed, propped the pillows a little and lay back with his hands folded on his chest.

'We got three possibilities here,' Burke said. 'One, she's a crazed fan and she wants your autograph. Two, she's part of a setup to catch you in a compromising situation with a white woman. Three, she's some kind of sex bomb with a thing for colored guys.'

'She ain't just a crazed fan,' Robinson said.

'So we look at possibilities two and three,' Burke said.

'Three,' Robinson said.

'Because?' Burke said.

Robinson turned from the window and sat on the other twin bed across from Burke. He leaned forward with his forearms on his thighs and his hands clasped.

'There's women like that,' Robinson said.

'The legend of the large black dick,' Burke said.

Robinson shrugged.

'That might be part of it,' Robinson said, 'but it's more than that. Women like that want you to be crude. They don't want no high-toned college Negro. They want a savage.'

Burke thought about Lauren.

'Why?' he said.

'I look like Sigmund Freud to you?' Robinson said.

'Not without a beard,' Burke said. 'The way some girls are crazy for horses? You know? Get to control a big powerful thing between their legs?'

'Don't know about horses,' Robinson said. 'But I know there's a certain kind of white woman that wants to do it with a big crude nigger and have him swear and talk dirty and shove her down and tear off her clothes.'

'And if the big crude nigger is also the most famous nigger in America?' Burke said.

'So much the better,' Robinson said.

'It could still be a setup,' Burke said.

Robinson nodded.

'Either way,' Burke said. 'I got to keep her away from you.'

'You're no fun at all,' Robinson said.

23

Smoking, Burke leaned on a lamppost in Kenmore Square across the sidewalk from the entrance to the hotel. He had the snapshot of Millicent. Behind him the weekend traffic, some of it from the recent ball game, moved inbound past him on Commonwealth Avenue. People came in and out of the hotel. The doorman hailed cabs, and opened doors, hustled bags, and pocketed fifty-cent tips. At quarter to seven Millicent got out of a cab wearing a sleeveless white sundress and a big straw hat, and carrying a big purse that matched the hat. The doorman jumped to hold the cab door, and scurried to open the hotel door as Millicent strode past him on very high heels. Burke stayed put until the cab she'd come in pulled away. He looked carefully around the square. He saw no one he recognized, no one who showed an interest in Millicent or where she was going. Burke snapped his cigarette butt into the gutter, and walked into the hotel.

Millicent was at the front desk. She took a big red envelope out of her purse and handed it to the desk clerk. He looked at it and nodded and put it under the counter. Millicent went to a chair in the lobby near the elevators and sat down, and showed a flash of thigh above her stockings as she crossed her legs. Burke admired the thigh. He knew she'd sit until the bellhop went past her with the red envelope. Then she'd follow him to Robinson's room. He looked around the lobby. No one was paying any attention to Millicent that wouldn't be explained by the amount of knee she was showing as she sat and waited. No one was looking at him, either.

Burke almost smiled. *Meet you there,* he said silently and

took the next elevator to the fifth floor. The room he shared with Robinson was empty. Burke poured himself a drink from a bottle of Vat 69 he'd brought with him. Then he closed the blinds, turned off the lights, put the .45 on the reading table by his elbow and sat in the one chair. He sipped his scotch and waited. In thirteen very slow minutes there was a knock on the door.

Burke said, 'Yeah?'

'Message for Mr Robinson.'

Burke stood, put his drink down, picked up the .45 and answered the door, keeping the .45 out of sight.

'Mr Robinson?'

'Sure,' Burke said.

He gave the bellhop a quarter and closed the door. He took the red envelope to the chair, put down the gun and opened the envelope. He picked up his drink and sipped it. There was no message in the envelope, only another snapshot. This one in the same bathing suit, back to the camera in her tight suit, looking awkwardly at the camera over her left shoulder. Burke recognized the Betty Grable pinup pose and smiled a little. Then he put the photo down beside the gun and drank a little scotch and waited some more. After another six minutes of slow time there was a soft knock on the door. Put down the drink. Pick up the gun. Walk to the door. Burke stood behind the door, out of sight when he opened it.

'Jackie?' a woman's voice said.

'Come in,' Burke said softly.

He knew he didn't sound like a Negro ballplayer from Pasadena, but neither, in fact, did Robinson. She turned toward him as she came into the dim room.

'Please,' she said, 'be gentle with... You aren't Jackie.'

Burke closed the door. Burke kept the gun against his right thigh, but she saw it.

'I'll scream,' she said.

'No,' Burke said. 'You start to scream and I'll knock you out flat cold on the floor.'

'What are you going to do with me?' she said.

Burke put the chain bolt on the door.

'We'll start by talking,' Burke said.

He pointed at the chair.

'Sit,' he said.

The room was small and Burke was big. Millicent had to maneuver around him to sit in the chair.

'You want a drink?' Burke said.

'No.'

She sat on the edge of the chair with her knees together and her hands clasped in her lap. She was wearing white gloves. Her perfume was heavy in the small room. Burke picked up his drink and sat near her on the edge of one of the beds.

'I, I'm sorry,' she said, 'to have seemed so scaredy. It's just that you startled me, and the gun...'

'Why'd you come here?' Burke said.

'Jackie invited me.'

'And gave you his room number?'

'Yes.'

'Which is why you pulled off that hocus-pocus with the red envelope.'

'I just wanted to send him a picture so he'd recognize me.'

'You wanted to follow the bellhop to his room,' Burke said. 'That's why you used a big red envelope, so you could spot it.'

'Oh dear,' she said.

Her voice was small and girlish with a husky edge to it.

'I was in the lobby when you came in,' Burke said.

'Oh, my,' she said. 'Maybe I could have a little teeny drink if you would.'

Burke poured her a shot in a water glass.

'Don't you have any ice or anything?' she said.

'Nope.'

She sighed in resignation and took the glass. She drank some scotch delicately. She smiled at Burke over the rim of the glass.

'I feel so unladylike,' she said, 'drinking it straight like this.'

Burke nodded. The .45 lay on the bed near his right hand.

'Are you going to do something to me?' Millicent said.

Burke sipped some scotch.

'We both know Mr Robinson didn't invite you here,' Burke said.

Millicent was looking around the room.

'Is this his room?' she said.

'His and mine.'

'Yours?'

'Yeah.'

'You room with Jackie?'

'Yeah.'

'I didn't… What is that like?'

Burke didn't say anything.

'Is some of this stuff his?' she said.

'Yes.'

'Which bed is his?'

'The one near the window,' Burke said.

Millicent put her hand out and rested it on the bed near the window. Burke wasn't sure she knew that she was doing it.

'Does he… ah… does he wear pajamas.'

'Pink ones,' Burke said, 'with little feet in them.'

'He doesn't really, does he?'

Burke shrugged. More and more she seemed to Burke like a woman eager to have sex with a famous black man.

'Anyone send you here?' Burke said.

'Send?'

'Send you here to get Mr Robinson in trouble.'

'I don't want to get Mr… Jackie in trouble.'

'Then you came here to fuck Mr Robinson,' Burke said.

'Don't be coarse.'

'What would be your explanation?' Burke said.

'I just love him.'

'You don't even know him.'

'But I watch him whenever he's in Boston and I go to New York to watch him. And I read about him in the papers.'

'Why?'

'He's so… beautiful.'

'Beautiful?'

'Yes,' she said.

She sat forward. Her eyes were bright. Her face under the makeup looked flushed.

'Beautiful like a black panther,' she said. 'Like a noble black stallion.'

Jesus Christ, Burke thought. *You can't fake that.* Millicent stopped suddenly.

'If he's not here,' she said, 'where is he?'

'Down the hall,' Burke said, 'playing cards with Clyde Sukeforth and Pee Wee Reese.'

'Will he come back here, soon?'

'I'll tell you what,' Burke said. 'You can't have Mr Robinson, but you can have the next best thing.'

'Best thing?'

'Yeah,' Burke said. 'I'll fuck you on his bed.'

She stared at him, her face now very definitely red.

'What a terrible thing to say to me,' she said and began to cry.

'You have no idea how terrible I can be,' Burke said.

'I want to go now,' she said.

'Sure,' Burke said. 'But if you come back, I will be really terrible.'

She stood, sobbing, her makeup already streaked with tears. She walked to the door.

'I never want to see you again,' she said as she took the chain bolt off.

'You won't have to, unless you bother Mr Robinson again.'

She took a breath and turned with the door ajar and looked at Burke.

'You are very cruel,' she said, trying to keep her voice steady.

'Keep it in mind,' Burke said.

She shook her head and went out the open door without closing it behind her. Burke walked to the doorway and watched her down the hall until the elevator came and took her away.

24

Jackie lay on the bed with his shirt off, reading the Boston American.

'A black panther,' Burke said. 'A beautiful black stallion.'

'Shut up,' Robinson said.

He continued to read the tabloid.

'That happen often?' Burke said.

He was still sipping Vat 69.

'You run into it,' Jackie said. 'Or you hear about it.'

'Happen to you before?'

'Yes.'

Jackie turned a page.

'The black stallion thing?' Burke said.

'All of us are supposed to be hung,' Jackie said. 'Some white women like that idea.'

Burke was silent for a moment. Then he took another small swallow of scotch.

'Got a lot of you killed,' Burke said.

Robinson put the paper down on his chest and looked at Burke.

'For looking at a white woman,' Robinson said. 'For smiling. For brushing her arm in a doorway. It's the big crime. Every Negro man knows it.'

'How about the white women?' Burke said.

'The ones want to crawl in bed with us? They got to know.'

'Maybe that's part of the fun,' Burke said.

' 'Course it is,' Robinson said. 'They like the thrill, you know? They're not just being bad, they're being bad with a nigger.'

'And they can get the nigger killed,' Burke said. 'How's that for being bad?'

Robinson nodded.

'It's a kind of a power, too,' he said. 'White woman with a black man... all she got to do is say he raped her.'

'She could do that to a white man,' Burke said.

Robinson smiled and didn't answer. Burke began to nod his head slowly.

'Not the same thing,' Burke said.

'Who's the last white man,' Robinson said, 'you can think of got lynched for rape?'

'Pretty sick,' Burke said.

'It is.'

'Easy way to set you up, too,' Burke said.

'I know. Why I was playing cards with two reputable white men when she came to my room.'

'I don't think this was a setup,' Burke said. 'I think Millicent was genuine.'

'She good-looking?' Robinson said.

'Yes.'

'Too bad. It's easier when they're not.'

Burke smiled a little.

'I offered on your behalf,' Burke said. 'But she wasn't interested.'

'The real thing or no thing,' Robinson said and picked up his newspaper again.

Burke was quiet sipping his scotch, looking out the window at Kenmore Square.

'Blackwell won another one,' Robinson said. 'Three-hitter against the Pirates.'

'I could throw a three-hitter against the Pirates,' Burke said.

'No you couldn't,' Robinson said.

They were quiet again. Robinson with the evening tabloid, Burke with his drink.

'It's not just white girls and Negroes,' Burke said after a time.

'No?'

'No. There are girls who go for men because they are…'

'Forbidden?'

'Something like that. They want the sex to be, dirty or something like that.'

'Like it would be with a big bad black Negro?'

'Or a bad sick white guy.'

'Puts us in nice company,' Robinson said.

'You know what I mean.'

'I do.'

Jackie smiled and lowered the paper enough so he could look at Burke over it.

'You got some personal experience?'

Burke was looking out the window, holding the water glass of scotch with both hands.

'Yeah,' he said. 'I think so.'

Robinson kept looking at him with the paper lowered again to his chest, but Burke had nothing else to say and after a while Robinson returned to the newspaper.

Box Score 5

Brooklyn.	AB.	H.	O.	A.	Boston.	AB.	H.	O.	A.
Stanky, 2b	5	1	2	5	Holmes, rf	5	2	3	0
Robinson, 1b	4	1	6	1	Hopp, cf	5	1	4	0
Reiser, cf	4	1	3	0	Torgeson, 1b	2	1	0	2
Furillo, lf	5	2	3	0	Elliott, 3b	4	1	2	0
Walker, rf	2	0	2	0	Rowell, lf	4	2	4	0
Lavagetto, 3b	3	0	4	1	Masi, c	4	2	6	0
Reese, ss	4	0	1	0	Sistl, ss	2	1	5	2
Bragan, c	3	0	3	1	Ryan, 2b	4	1	3	1
*Rackley	0	0	0	0	Spahn, p	4	0	0	1
Barney, p	3	1	0	0		—	—	—	—
Casey, p	0	0	0	0	Totals	34	11	27	6
†Miksis	1	0	0	0					
	—	—	—	—					
Totals	34	6	24	8					

```
Brooklyn ....................0 2 0   0 0 0   0 0 1—3
Boston ......................0 0 0   0 0 2   4 0 *—6
```

*Ran for Bragan in ninth. †Batted for Casey in ninth. R—Reese, Rackley, Barney. Holmes, Hopp, Torgeson 2. Elliott, Rowell. E—Torgeson, Elliott. RBI—Barney, Stanky, Rowell, Elliott 2. Masi 3. 2B —Furillo, Barney, Hopp, Masi. SB—Reiser, Rowell, Masi. DP—Lavagetto, Stanky and Robinson. BB —Barney 3, Casey 2. Spahn 6. SO—Barney 1, Casey 1, Spahn 4. Hits—Barney 3 in 6 1-3. HP— Casey 1. B—Casey. Loser—Barney.

Bobby

One of my most vivid memories is of my mother screaming for my father. His name was Gus and when she needed him she would elongate that single syllable in a way hard to describe. The emergency was rarely dire. She would scream for my father if there was a mouse, or if the dog threw up, or if something started to boil over on the stove, or the car wouldn't start, or a zipper got stuck, or a window wouldn't close, or a door wouldn't open. He was always calm when he responded and always able to correct the thing and allow my mother to go right back to being what she was most of the time, which is to say bossy and full of herself. Often wrong, my father would sometimes remark, but never uncertain.

I always enjoyed these moments of my father's domestic heroism, because so much of the time my mother was everywhere telling everyone what to do. And he was letting her as if he didn't mind.

They had been married sixteen years in 1947 and I don't recall ever seeing them fight. They would annoy one another occasionally. She would raise her finger and speak forcefully. He would turn and walk away with no expression. But the door would close very firmly behind him. It was unwise to make my mother mad. She didn't get over it easily and would sulk and sigh for days.

My father went to work each morning in his suit and came home each evening. He would take off his suit jacket and his tie, roll back his cuffs, and have a drink while supper was cooking. We would eat at the kitchen table and both of them were attentive to what I had to say.

When I was small, and they went out together on Saturday nights, and my mother came home, bubbling with laughter and smelling deliciously of perfume and cocktails, she would sit on my bed, while my father took the babysitter home, and tell me what they'd done. At those moments she seemed unutterably glamorous and I felt deeply lucky that she was my mother.

By the time I was fifteen, I believe I knew one person who had been divorced, the mother of a friend, who I felt must feel deeply ashamed. I was always startled to hear any reference to it. Divorce happened in Hollywood. And it didn't seem to matter. Filtered through the gossip prism, no hint of genuine feeling was attached to it. I knew nothing of adultery. I knew it existed because there was a commandment against it. But in practical terms it was impossible that someone's wife, or mother, would have sexual intercourse with another man outside of marriage. Married sex was difficult enough.

For all of us, though some of us must have seen evidence to the contrary, it was assumed that marriage was a happy condition that lasted a lifetime.

And I never knew anyone who wasn't eager to have his turn at it.

25

Robinson and Burke ate breakfast in midtown Manhattan at a restaurant called the Virginian, which featured omelets cooked in the front window. A few people were gathered on the sidewalk to watch.

'Who the Giants pitching today?' Burke said.

'Koslo.'

'You hit him?'

'I hit him good,' Robinson said.

As they were eating two men came in and stopped inside the door one on either side. The one to the left wore a blue seersucker suit that didn't fit him well. The one on the right had on a well-tailored tan Palm Beach suit. He wore a low crowned straw fedora with a snap brim and a big colorful band. The door opened again and a tall graceful man with white hair and a strong nose came in and walked to the table where Robinson and Burke were sitting.

'May I join you?' the man said.

Robinson looked up and didn't answer.

Burke said, 'Why?'

'My name is Frank Boucicault. I'd like to speak to you about my son.'

'Mr Robinson and I are having breakfast,' Burke said.

'If you'd prefer he not hear what I have to say, we might ask him to step outside,' Boucicault said.

'We won't do that,' Burke said.

'What I have to say involves Lauren Roach,' Boucicault said.

'Burke,' Jackie said. 'Be okay, you want me to step out.'

Burke shook his head.

'What about her?' he said to Boucicault.

Boucicault looked at Robinson for a moment, then at Burke. He rubbed his hands gently together.

'She is engaged to my son,' he said.

Burke didn't speak.

'I know she was with you for a time. I know you've had trouble with my son about it.'

'Not much trouble,' Burke said.

'No. My son is not a tough guy. He thinks he is. But he isn't.'

Boucicault was quiet again. He kept rubbing his hands. Robinson was quiet, his dark eyes fixed on Boucicault. No one was eating.

'On the other hand,' he said, 'I am.'

'Me too,' Burke said.

'I know. You killed two of my people.'

'I did.'

'But you did not kill my son. That buys you something.'

'But not everything,' Burke said.

Boucicault smiled.

'No,' he said. 'Not everything.'

He stopped rubbing his hands and pressed them together and rested the fingertips against the point of his chin.

'My son, Mr Burke, is not what I had in mind when he was born. But that makes him no less my son. I love him, and I will see to it that he has in life what he wants from it. That includes the Roach girl.'

'Unless she doesn't want him,' Burke said.

'I don't care what she wants,' Boucicault said. 'And you shouldn't either. Maybe you're good. The men you killed were pretty good. Doesn't matter. I could send a hundred better.'

Burke drank some coffee.

'I don't want the Roach girl,' Burke said.

'Good,' Boucicault said. 'The other thing is for you to stay away from Louis.'

'I got no interest in Louis,' Burke said.

Robinson had finished his breakfast. He was sipping a second cup of coffee, his eyes shifting from one speaker to the other.

'I'll try to keep him away from you,' Boucicault said.

'Be a good thing,' Burke said.

'I care about appearances,' Boucicault said. 'I started in a garbage heap, and I crawled out of it, and over the years I have learned to speak well, and dress properly, and carry myself with dignity.'

Burke didn't speak.

'But you should not be fooled. My resources are great, and I have no more scruples than a cannibal.'

'Sure,' Burke said.

The two men looked at each other.

'You're not scared of me,' Boucicault said. 'You should be, but you're not.'

Burke shrugged again.

'Why aren't you?' Boucicault said.

Burke finished the last of his eggs, and wiped his mouth carefully with a napkin.

'Things don't matter much to me,' he said.

Boucicault looked at Robinson.

'You got any thoughts on this, boy?'

Robinson's face went blank. His gaze flattened.

'No thoughts,' he said.

'Keep it just that way,' Boucicault said.

He looked at Burke.

'We clear?' he said.

Burke nodded slowly.

'Your kid is sick,' Burke said.

The lines at the corners of Boucicault's mouth deepened.

'I know that,' he said.

'Something wrong with the girl,' Burke said.

'I know that, too.'

'They probably make each other sicker,' Burke said.

'I do what I can,' Boucicault said. 'I just want you to stay clear.'

'Glad to,' Burke said.

26

Burke drove Robinson to the Polo Grounds. He liked to go up the West Side, along the Hudson River, and then east to the top of Manhattan, where the ballpark stood, under Coogan's Bluff, across the Harlem River from Yankee Stadium.

'He called you boy,' Burke said.

Robinson nodded.

'And you took it,' Burke said.

'Got to take it,' Robinson said.

'I know.'

Across the Hudson River, the Palisades rose implacably.

'Is it worth it?' Burke said.

'What's "it"?'

'Name calling,' Burke said. 'Death threats, getting thrown at, getting spiked, me?'

'You're all right,' Jackie said.

'Thanks.'

'The rest of it? Yeah, it's bad. But it's an extension, you know. It's an extension of Negro life. Same thing go on if I try to live in the wrong neighborhood, or eat in the wrong restaurant, or go to the wrong school, or date the wrong woman.'

'White woman.'

'Yeah. So there's nothing new going on here. Just getting more attention than it usually does.'

'Hard being colored,' Burke said.

'I got Rachel,' Robinson said.

'Rachel?'

'My wife.'

'I didn't know you were married,' Burke said.

'You been out to my house,' Jackie said. 'You picked me up at my house this morning.'

'I never been in, for all I knew you were living in there with a billy goat.'

'Been married now a year and a half. She's at every home game.'

'I wasn't looking for young Negro women,' Burke said.

'No, 'course not.'

'Thing like this must be hard on a marriage,' Burke said.

'Can tear it apart,' Robinson said.

'How you doing?'

'Makes us tighter,' Robinson said. 'Her and me. We doing this together.'

'What the hell is it exactly you're doing?'

'Integrating the great American pastime.'

'Yeah. I know all the stuff I read. But what is it that *you* are doing, yourself?'

'I'm playing at a level I'm good enough to play at. I'm making a little money. I'm getting famous. I'm proving to the bastards that I can play. I'm making Rachel proud.'

Burke thought about this for a moment.

'And,' Burke said, 'you're integrating baseball.'

'I am.'

'Rachel matters?'

'More than all the rest,' Jackie said.

'Because you love her,' Burke said.

'Because we love each other,' Jackie said.

Burke shook his head.

'You buy it all, don't you?' he said. 'Love, equality, the great American game.'

'Gotta buy something,' Jackie said. 'Whadda you buy?'

'Lucky Strikes,' Burke said. 'Vat 69.'

'That's all?'

'Money's good. I like to get laid.'

They turned east through Harlem.

'You ever been married?' Jackie said.

'Yeah.'

'Now you're not.'

'Nope.'

'Divorce?'

Burke nodded.

'What about this Lauren?' Jackie said.

'I guarded her before I guarded you.'

'Anything else?'

'There was something else,' Burke said.

'What happened?'

Burke shrugged.

'She one of those women you talking about?' Jackie said.

'Got a thing for the wrong men?'

Everyone on the street as Burke drove toward the Polo Grounds was Negro. Colored women sat together on the front stairs of elegant old brownstone houses, watching the street life, interested.

'You in the war?' Jackie said.

'Yeah.'

'Bad?'

'Yeah.'

Jackie nodded.

There were children playing stickball. They moved reluctantly as Burke drove slowly past. He didn't answer Jackie's question.

'Bad,' Jackie said. 'How'd you feel 'bout this Lauren woman?'

Burke shrugged again. Jackie looked at him for a silent moment.

'You don't know? Or you don't want to say?'

'I got no feelings,' Burke said.

'You ever have any?' Jackie said.

'Before the war,' Burke said.

'Was it the war or the wife,' Jackie said, 'wiped you out?'

'Both.'

It was warm. The windows were down. Burke could smell the tar and steam heat smell of the city. The dark Negro eyes on the street watched him as he drove past. *Stranger in a strange land.*

'So she have the hots for you?' Robinson said.

Burke shrugged.

'You turn her down, she hooks up with Boucicault's son?'

'Something like that.'

'He bad?'

'Sick bad,' Burke said.

'And you don't care?' Jackie said.

Burke shrugged. He braked for a red light.

''Cause you got no feelings,' Jackie said.

'This is none of your fucking business,' Burke said.

'See,' Jackie said. 'You do have feelings.'

'I feel like you're a fucking asshole,' Burke said.

The two men looked at each other for a moment. Robinson was trying not to smile, and failing. Then Burke smiled with him.

'A fucking dark Sigmund Freud,' Burke said.

They were both laughing when the light changed and they made the turn to the Polo Grounds.

Box Score 6

Brooklyn.	AB.	H.	O.	A.	New York.	AB.	H.	O.	A.
Stanky, 2b	5	2	1	3	Blattner, 2b	3	1	4	7
Robinson, 1b	5	4	6	2	Kress, ss	5	2	1	5
Reese, ss	3	1	3	2	Gearhart, cf	5	3	2	0
Furillo, cf	4	1	2	0	Mize, 1b	4	1	13	1
Walker, rf	4	0	2	0	Marshall, rf	4	4	1	0
Edwards, c	4	1	4	0	Lombardi, c	5	0	4	2
Jorgensen, 3b	4	1	2	0	Gordon, lf	3	1	0	0
Hermanski, lf	1	1	0	0	Lohrke, 3b	3	1	1	4
Miksis, lf	2	1	3	0	Koslo, p	2	0	1	0
Gregg, p	3	0	1	2	Trinkle, p	2	0	0	0
Dockins, p	0	0	0	0					
*Snider	1	0	0	0					
					Totals	36	13	27	19
Totals	36	12	24	9					

```
Brooklyn .................. 1 0 1   0 1 0   0 0 2—5
New York .................. 2 1 0   0 0 0   0 6 *—9
```

*Batted for Dockins in ninth. R—Stanky 2, Robinson, Hermanski, Miksis, Blattner 2, Kerr 2, Gearhart, Mize, Marshall, Gordon, Lohrke. E—Lombardi, Hermanski, Jorgensen, Reese. RBI—Reese 2, Gearhart 2, Marshall 2, Blattner, Robinson, Gordon, Kerr, Mize 2, Stanky 2. 2B—Hermanski, Jorgensen. HR—Gordon, Mize, Marshall, Stanky. SB—Robinson 2, Gordon, Blattner 2, Kerr. BB—Gregg 5. Koslo 2. NO—Gregg 3, Koslo 2, Trinkle 1. Hits—Koslo 8 in 5 1-3, Gregg 11 in 7 2-3. Winner —Trinkle. Loser—Gregg. Umpires—Gore, Pinelli and Barlick. Attendance—52,147.

27

The Dodgers had lost a night game, at home, to the Phillies. Jackie had tripled off Ken Heintzelman and been thrown out at the plate trying to steal home. Now, after midnight, in light traffic, Burke drove Jackie home.

'You were white,' Burke said, 'you could have run over Seminick.'

'Not this year.'

'Next year?'

'Maybe.'

'Year after?' Burke said.

'Sooner or later,' Jackie said.

'You really believe that?' Burke said.

'Yes.'

'You think the day will come when you can run into somebody blocking the plate and it won't cause trouble?'

'Yes.'

'You think that they're going to like you?'

Robinson turned his head toward Burke. It was too dark for Burke to see his eyes, but he knew the look. He'd seen it before.

'Don't care if they like me,' Jackie said. 'But I can play this game and I'm going to ram it down their throats until they get used to it.'

There was a set of headlights behind them that seemed to Burke to have been there for a while. Past the next street-light Burke slowed a little and watched in the rearview mirror. The car was a gray 1946 Ford sedan. Burke made no comment but as they drove he kept track of the gray Ford behind them.

'Who knows where you live?' Burke said. 'Besides me.'

'Rachel knows,' Jackie said.

'And your mother probably knows,' Burke said. 'I mean outside of family.'

'Mr Rickey,' Robinson said.

'And?'

'That's all,' Jackie said. 'Shotton has my phone number, but no address. Why are you asking?'

'Just wondered,' Burke said.

'Why you wondering?'

'I'm supposed to wonder,' Burke said. 'I'm your fucking bodyguard.'

'Oh,' Jackie said. 'Yeah.'

The gray Ford was still with them when Burke pulled up in front of Robinson's house. The front porch light was on and there was a light in the downstairs window on the right.

'She's waiting up,' Burke said.

'Yeah. We usually have a cup of tea together when I get home.'

The gray Ford went slowly past them and turned right at the next corner. There were at least two men in it. Burke thought they were white.

'If she goes to all the home games,' Burke said, 'why doesn't she ever ride home with us?'

'She goes with some other wives,' Jackie said.

'The wives get along?'

'Some,' Jackie said. 'Mr Rickey's worried 'bout us together in public. Somebody insults her and I…' Robinson spread his hands.

Burke nodded.

'I'll walk you to the door,' he said.

Robinson glanced at him sharply.

'What's up?'

'All part of the service.'

'The hell it is,' Jackie said. 'You worried about something.'

'I thought I spotted a car following us here. It went on by, and I don't see it now.'

'Rachel,' Jackie said.

'You go on in,' Burke said. 'Lock the door. If anyone tries to get in call the cops. I'll hang around out here for a while.'

Jackie was silent for a moment. Then he nodded. They got out of the car and began to walk to his house. The summer night was still, except for some insect noise and an occasional traffic sound.

At the door Jackie said, 'Be careful.'

'I was born for this,' Burke said.

Jackie nodded and went into his house. Burke stood until he heard the bolt slide, then he turned and went slowly back to his car. The gray Ford was not in sight. Burke drove his car two blocks down and wedged it in on a hydrant. He went to the trunk and took out a shotgun with both barrels sawn short. He opened it, put two shells in it, snapped the breech closed and began to walk back toward Jackie's house with the shotgun held down next to his right leg. He stayed inconspicuously close to the cars parked on each side of the street.

Across the street from Jackie's house, he sat on the curb, in the shadows between the bumpers of two parked cars, with the butt of the shotgun on the pavement between his legs, and the barrel cradled in his left arm. He kicked off his shoes. The street stayed empty. No cars moved on it. No people walked beside it. One yellow cat crossed it with little rapid steps that made no sound, and disappeared into some shrubs along the foundation of the house next door to Jackie's. There was no wind. No insect sound. No night birds. No more cats. Dogs didn't bark. No music. No domestic disturbance. Burke was motionless. He knew he could sit like this as long as he had to. He'd done it in the war. Part of the trick was to relax into it. No focus, absorb it. Let the situation soak into you.

From his right, up the street, a car came slowly toward him with its lights out. As it passed under the streetlight, he saw that it was a gray Ford sedan. It was very quiet, as if the engine had been shut off and the car was gliding in neutral. It stopped a house short of Jackie's. No one got out. Burke sat still breathing gently through his nose. It was a two-door sedan with a black and yellow New York State license tag. After a while two men got out of the front seat of the Ford. One from the driver's side, one from the passenger's side. The man who got out the passenger's side was carrying a small canvas bag. Burke wondered if there was anyone left in the car. It would make sense for them to leave a driver, but one of the men had come out from the driver's side. Three people weren't going to ride around for a while crammed into the front seat, while the back seat was empty. So if there was anyone, he was in the back seat and why would he stay there sitting in the back seat while the other men went to work?

The two men started across the neighboring front lawn walking toward the corner of Jackie's house. When they reached it they turned toward the back, away from the streetlights. Burke stood and walked quietly across the street, past the Ford sedan, after them. Nothing happened. He made no sound as he walked in his stocking feet across Jackie's neat grass lawn, and down along the side of Jackie's house. In the shadow of the house, away from the streetlight, Burke stopped and listened while his pupils dilated. He could hear movement very slightly, and then as his eyes adjusted he could see the two men in vague shape gathered together at the back door. Burke moved closer. One of the men held a big revolver in his hand. The other had taken a flat bar from the canvas bag. Burke moved closer, his left shoulder brushing the house. There was no more relaxing into it. Now it was all focus, the two men and himself. Nothing else existed. The man with the flat bar whispered to the man with the gun. The sound in the night was shocking. The man with the gun whispered back. Burke was only ten feet away. He cocked both hammers on the shotgun. Both the men straightened and whirled toward the sound.

With his back pressed to the house, aiming at them across his body, Burke said, 'Shotgun, both barrels.' The men hesitated. 'Ten-gauge,' Burke said. 'Cut both of you in two.' The men stared into the darkness trying to see. He was too close. From where he was, with a double-barreled ten-gauge, he couldn't miss. Who was with him? 'Drop the gun or I'll kill you,' Burke said. The man with the gun hesitated, then decided. He turned suddenly, bringing the gun up, and Burke shot him in the chest with one barrel. The man made a sound of air suddenly expelled and went three feet backward and fell on his back. 'Okay,' the man with the flat bar said. 'Okay.' He put his hands in the air.

Burke saw movement at the window.

'Don't come out,' he yelled. 'Don't call the cops. Don't do anything.'

With the shotgun pushed up against the underside of the man's chin Burke took a handgun from a holster on the man's right hip. He dropped the gun into the canvas bag, put the flat bar in there as well.

'Okay,' he said. 'Drag your pal to the car and stick him in the trunk.'

'He's too fucking heavy.'

Burke jabbed the muzzle of the shotgun against the man's cheek.

'Ow,' the man said and put his hand to his face.

'Do it, or I'll drag you both.'

The man stooped down, got hold of his friend's arms and began to drag him toward the Ford. Burke followed him. No lights went on in the neighborhood. No police cars roared up to the house. You could fire off an anti-aircraft gun in most neighborhoods, Burke thought, and no one would call the cops. They wouldn't know it was an anti-aircraft gun. Just a loud noise. *Go back to sleep, Edna.* The man struggled to get the body in the trunk and by the time he finally succeeded he and the rear end of the Ford were smeared with blood.

'Close the trunk,' Burke said.

He did.

'You drive,' Burke said.

He kept the shotgun level until the man slipped into the driver's seat, then he got into the passenger's seat, put the canvas bag on the floor, and lay the still-cocked shotgun across his lap with the barrel pointing at the driver.

'Where?' the man said.

His voice was hoarse.

'Straight until I tell you something else,' Burke said.

The man put the keys in the ignition, pressed the starter button, put the car in gear and drove.

28

The man stared straight ahead, as he drove slowly, without speaking. Burke watched him for a moment. He was a thick pale-faced man with a lot of flesh around his neck. He was wearing a tan golf jacket and a white broadcloth shirt. He was having trouble swallowing. Burke was silent. No cars passed them as they drove. As they went under a streetlight Burke could see the sweat on the man's face. In the quiet night with only the sound of the tires on the pavement, Burke could hear how shallow the man's breathing was.

There was a bus stop past a gas station on the right.

'Pull over,' Burke said. 'Leave the motor on.'

The man pulled in and stopped in the empty space of the bus stop.

'I might not kill you,' Burke said.

The man didn't answer.

'I want to kill you,' Burke said. 'You would have killed me back there if you could have.'

The man shook his head.

'But I need something from you,' Burke said. 'So I might have to let you go.'

The man turned and looked at him.

'If you got it and give it to me,' Burke said.

The man nodded.

'What's your name?' Burke said.

The man cleared his throat.

'Richard,' he said.

Burke nodded as if a suspicion had been confirmed.

'Okay, Richard,' Burke said, 'here's how it is. You give me what I want and I let you go. Or you don't – because you won't, because you can't, makes no difference to me – and I cut you in two with the shotgun and dump you in the trunk on top of your buddy.'

'Whaddya want?' Richard said.

'What were you doing at that house?'

'I don't know. I just went along with Chuck, for backup, you know?'

'Richard,' Burke said, 'you don't seem to get your situation here. If that's the kind of answers you can give me, you're going to be dead in maybe a minute.'

Richard looked down at the steering wheel and shook his head as if to clear it.

'We was going to kill the nigger,' he said.

'Why?'

'Guy wanted him dead.'

'What guy?'

'I can't tell you that,' Richard said.

Burke laughed softly. He put the muzzle of the shotgun against Richard's right cheekbone.

"I can't. I rat and I'm a dead man.'

'And if you don't?' Burke said softly.

Richard was silent for a moment, shaking his head slowly, staring at the empty street. Burke could see tears on his cheeks.

'Was it Paglia?' Burke said.

Richard nodded slowly.

'He hire you himself?' Burke said.

Richard shook his head.

'Who?' Burke said.

'Cash.' Richard was almost whispering.

'Tall thin guy?'

Richard nodded.

'Paglia's shooter?' Burke said. 'Sort of high shoulders?'

Richard nodded again, crying silently.

'How do you get in touch with him?' Burke said.

Richard started to shake his head. Burke jabbed his cheek with the shotgun.

'I…' Richard said. 'I… You call a joint on the West Side, the Black Cat Club, leave a message with the bartender.'

'And Cash calls you back?'

'Yeah, or he meets you someplace.'

Burke nodded. He sat quietly for a moment.

Then he said, 'Okay, drive back the way you came.'

'U-turn?' Richard said.

'Yeah.'

'What if there's a cop?'

'Make the fucking U-turn,' Burke said.

They drove in silence back along the empty street. Two blocks from Robinson's house, Burke said, 'Stop here.'

The car stopped next to the hydrant where Burke had parked his car. Burke opened his door and put the canvas bag out onto the street.

'You're on your own,' he said to Richard.

'What am I supposed to do with Chuck?' Richard said.

'Not my problem,' Burke said. 'I was you I'd dump the car, get on a train and go live someplace else.'

He stepped out of the car, and shut the door. He watched as Richard pulled away, then he picked up the canvas bag, put it in his trunk, took the remaining load from the shotgun, put the shell in his pocket and the shotgun in the trunk. He closed the lid. Then he walked the two blocks to Robinson's house and rang the doorbell. There was movement in the house and at the window, then Robinson opened the front door. He was dressed and he carried a baseball bat.

'Everything's fine,' Burke said.

'How about the shot I heard?'

Burke shook his head.

'Everything's fine,' he said. 'Go to sleep. I'll pick you up in the morning.'

Burke stared back at Robinson's dark fierce intelligent gaze for a moment, and waited. But Robinson decided not to say anything else. He closed the door. Burke walked back two blocks to his car and drove home.

Box Score 7

Phila'phia.	AB.	H.	O.	A.	Brooklyn.	AB.	H.	O.	A.
H. Walker, cf	4	1	3	0	Stanky, 2b	5	2	5	1
Verban, 2b	4	1	3	2	Robinson, 1b	4	0	10	0
Ennis, lf	4	1	1	0	Reiser, lf	5	2	3	0
Wyrostek, rf	4	1	3	0	F. Walker, rf	4	2	1	0
Seminick, c	4	2	8	1	Furillo, cf	5	2	4	0
Tabor, 3b	4	0	1	0	Edwards, c	4	3	4	0
Schultz, 1b	4	1	4	0	Jorgensen, 3b	4	1	0	2
Newsome, ss	3	1	1	3	Reese, ss	2	1	0	3
Leonard, p	2	0	0	1	Branca, p	4	0	0	1
*Gilbert	1	0	0	0					
Schanz, p	0	0	0	1	Totals	37	13	27	7
Totals	34	8	24	8					

```
Philadelphia .............. 000   000   000—0
Brooklyn .................. 010   012   01*—5
```

*Batted for Leonard in eighth. R—Stanky, Robinson, F. Walker, Edwards, Reese. E—Verban, Seminick, Newsome. Edwards. RBI—Furillo. Stanky, F. Walker. 2B—F. Walker, Newsome, Furillo, Jorgensen. 3B—H. Walker, SB—Wyrostek, Furillo, Robinson. DP—Seminick, Verban and Seminick; Reese, Stanky and Robinson. BB—Leonard 3, Schanz 1. SO—Leonard 4. Schanz 1. Branca 3. Hits—Leonard 12 in 7. WP—Branca. Loser—Leonard. Umpires—Barr, Jorda and Conian. Attendance—32,170.

122

29

They were on their way to a home game with the Reds. Burke was driving.

'They came to my home,' Robinson said. 'They know where we live.'

'Just two of them,' Burke said. 'One of them is dead and the other one is running away.'

'You're sure he's running?'

'He told me that Paglia sent him. When Paglia finds out he'll have him killed, if he can find him.'

'And this guy knows that?' Jackie said.

'Yes.'

Jackie nodded.

'How's Paglia going to find out?' he said.

'I'm going to tell him,' Burke said.

'Why?'

'This needs to stop,' Burke said. 'I'm going to talk with Paglia.'

'You think you can?'

'Yeah.'

'What are you going to say?'

'I'll think of something,' Burke said.

Jackie started to speak, and stopped, and looked thoughtfully at Burke.

'We knew it would be tough,' Jackie said. 'Me and Rachel, when we signed on. I don't think we knew it would be this tough.'

'Nobody knew,' Burke said.

'She has to be safe,' Jackie said.

'She'll be all right,' Burke said. 'It's sort of against the rules to kill wives and children.'

'Rules?'

Burke nodded.

'You think they got in, they wouldn't have hurt her?' Jackie said.

'They weren't supposed to.'

'How do you know?'

'I know a lot of thugs,' Burke said.

'And they have rules?'

'Sure. Most people got rules.'

'You?' Jackie said.

'Except me,' Burke said.

Jackie stared at Burke for a moment. It was what Burke had come to think of as *the look*. Jackie didn't say anything and Burke wheeled the car into the players' parking lot. They walked to the clubhouse in silence. When Jackie was inside, Burke went around and in through the rotunda to sit in his place by the dugout.

30

It was the sixth inning. The Reds led the Dodgers 9–1. Bucky Walters was pitching. Augie Galen had a three-run home run, and Grady Hatton had two doubles. For the Dodgers, Vic Lombardi had given way to Hank Behrman, who had been replaced by Clyde King. Jackie had a single and a stolen base. Burke was drinking Coca-Cola, watching the ever-hopeful Hilda Chester ring her cowbell from the outfield stands. A tall thin man with high shoulders came down the aisle and slid into the seat next to him.

'You want to talk with me?' he said.

'Cash,' Burke said.

'Okay, Burke, you know my name.'

Burke smiled a little.

'And you know mine,' he said.

'I've known yours for a long time, remember?'

'And now we're even,' Burke said.

'Okay, we're buddies,' Cash said. 'What do you want?'

'You're still with Paglia?' Burke said.

Cash nodded. His eyes were a very light blue. It made his face seem almost artificial.

'And you sent Richard and Chuck to kill Robinson,' Burke said.

Cash made no answer.

'Did you know they tried to break into his house?'

Cash didn't speak.

'His wife was there.'

Cash shrugged.

'You think they wouldn't have killed her too?'

Cash shrugged again.

It was the first half of the seventh inning. Frankie Baumholtz singled into right field on the ground between Jackie and Eddie Stanky.

'What makes you think I got anything to do with that?' Cash said.

'Richard told me.'

'And Chuck?'

'Chuck's dead,' Burke said.

Cash nodded slowly.

'Where's Richard?' he said.

'Out of town,' Burke said.

'I know why,' Cash said.

Eddie Miller hit into a double play. Cash gestured at a vendor as he came down the aisle toward them.

'You want another Coca-Cola?' Cash said.

'Sure.'

Cash held up two fingers, got the Coca-Colas, handed one to Burke, put the other one on the floor and paid the vendor. Then he picked up his drink and leaned back and put his feet up against the railing in front of him. He looked at the field.

'You think anybody ever hit that Abe Stark sign out there and got a free suit?'

'Only if the right fielder fell down,' Burke said.

Cash drank some of his Coke.

'Damn sign's three feet off the ground,' Cash said.

Babe Young flied to Pete Reiser in left field, and the teams changed sides. Cash drank again. Then he took a package of Camels from his shirt pocket, offered one to Burke, took one for himself and lit Burke's and his own with a silver Zippo. He took in a long drag and then spoke as he let the smoke out slowly.

'I didn't know about the wife,' he said.

Burke sipped his soda.

'Hard to get good help,' Cash said. 'Since the war.'

'You in it?' Burke said.

'North Africa,' Cash said. 'You?'

'Guadalcanal.'

Gene Hermanski hit for King and singled.

'You ask me to meet you so we could swap war stories?' Cash said.

'We need to work this out,' Burke said. 'I don't want to have to keep shooting people.'

'We got plenty.'

'We need to work this out,' Burke said.

'You got a suggestion?'

'I need a little time,' Burke said.

'So?'

'I want you to give it to me.'

'Talk to Paglia,' Cash said. 'I don't call the shots.'

'I want to talk with Paglia, but not yet,' Burke said. 'I need a week or so.'

'I work for Paglia,' Cash said.

'If Paglia wants something done he tells you and you take care of it.'

'Yeah.'

'So he wants to send somebody else after us, he'll tell you and you stall it for a week,' Burke said.

'Why would I do that?'

'You put the wife in danger.'

'Yeah?'

'You broke the rules,' Burke said.

Cash smiled.

'I thought you didn't care about anything,' Cash said.

'I do what I'm hired for.'

'Me too,' Cash said.

'Can you give me a week I don't have to be looking around every corner?'

Cash looked at him silently, nodding his head slowly. Eddie Stanky, on a 3–1 pitch, fouled out to Ray Lamanno. Cash grinned suddenly. There was a wolfish quality to the grin.

'Sure,' Cash said. 'Why not?'

31

Burke called Julius Roach from a pay phone near the clubhouse door.

'Nice to hear your voice again, Burke. What can I do for you?'

'I need to talk with whatever colored guy runs the rackets in Harlem.'

'And you think I would know?' Roach said.

'Yes sir.'

'Would you care to tell me why you want this?'

'No sir.'

There was silence on the other end of the phone for a moment.

Then Roach said, 'Call me tomorrow.'

'Thank you.'

Again silence.

'Have you heard at all from my daughter?' Roach said.

'No.'

Silence.

'She all right?' Burke said finally.

'Certainly,' Roach said.

'Give her my best.'

'No,' Roach said. 'I don't think I will.'

'I'll call you tomorrow,' Burke said.

Burke closed his eyes and stood with the phone still in his hand for a long time after Roach hung up. He pressed his shoulder blades against the wall and rolled the back of his head slowly back and forth on the concrete, until Jackie showed up.

'How long you been with your wife?' Burke said to Jackie as they drove home.

'Met her in 1941,' Jackie said. 'We were both at UCLA.'

'You been together since?'

'Yes. Got married 'bout a year and a half ago.'

'Any regrets?' Burke said.

'It's the greatest thing I ever did,' he said. 'Who we talking about here?'

Burke shook his head.

'We talking about you and that girl that likes bad men?'

'What the fuck do you know?' Burke said.

Jackie smiled.

'Hell,' he said. 'I been to college.'

Burke snorted. They drove in silence for a time, until Jackie spoke again.

'What if you turned out not to be so bad a guy as you think you are?'

Burke shrugged.

'And she liked you anyway?'

Burke shrugged again.

'I don't want to talk about it,' he said.

'You brought it up,' Jackie said.

'I just asked about your wife.'

'Sure,' Jackie said. 'I guess that's right.'

32

Wendell Jackson had an office in the back of a pool room on Seventh Avenue near 131st Street. There were three Negroes playing pool when Burke entered. All three looked at him without comment.

'Looking for Wendell Jackson,' Burke said to them.

They paid no attention to him. Burke walked past them to the back of the pool room and knocked on a closed door beside the Coke machine. It was opened by a well-built light-skinned

Negro with a thin mustache. He was wearing an expensive tan double-breasted suit, a white on white shirt, a hand-painted tie and a Borsolino hat. He looked at Burke without speaking, his body blocking the door opening.

'I'd like to talk with Wendell Jackson,' Burke said.

'Un huh.'

The Negro didn't move.

'Julius Roach sent me,' Burke said.

The Negro looked silently at Burke for a time. Then he closed the door. Burke waited. In maybe a minute, the door opened again. The Negro stepped aside and Burke went in. There was another Negro. He was slender and much darker than the man who'd opened the door. He had receding hair and wore a white shirt with loose sleeves, and high-waisted gray slacks and sandals. The shirt was unbuttoned over his smooth hard chest. He was half lying on a chaise drinking iced tea. He gestured Burke toward a straight-backed chair beside a desk. The light-skinned Negro closed the office door and leaned on the wall beside it with his arms folded over his chest. Burke sat in the straight chair.

'I'm Wendell,' the dark-skinned man said. He stressed the second syllable.

'My name's Burke.'

'You want some tea, Burke?'

'Sure.'

'Ellis?'

The light-skinned Negro went to a refrigerator in the corner of the room and took out a pitcher and poured some tea into a tall glass. He put the glass on the desk next to Burke and went back to his space beside the door.

'Hope you like it sweet,' Jackson said.

'It's fine,' Burke said.

'I like it with a little fresh mint,' Jackson said.

'Sure,' Burke said.

'So what does Julius want?' Jackson said.

Burke shook his head.

'It's what I want.'

Jackson raised his eyebrows and tipped his head a little.

'Honest to God?' Jackson said.

'I asked Julius who ran the rackets up here, and he sent me to you.'

'How you know Julius?'

'Used to be his daughter's bodyguard,' Burke said.

Jackson smiled and drank some tea.

'So you the gentleman snapped a couple of Frank's boys.'

'Yes.'

'Had a little problem with young Louis, I think.'

'I did,' Burke said. 'Now I don't.'

'You bodyguarding Julius's daughter,' Jackson said. 'You protecting her from people or people from her?'

'Either way,' Burke said. 'Now I'm guarding Jackie Robinson.'

'Goddamn,' Jackson said. 'You hear that, Ellis? This is the man guarding Jackie.'

Ellis nodded silently.

'So you be the guy had the blowout with Johnny Paglia over on one two five?'

'Yes,' Burke said.

'Man, you do get about, do you not?' Jackson said.

'You pay attention,' Burke said.

'Happened in my neighborhood,' Jackson said. 'You didn't fool with no sissies.'

'Luck of the draw,' Burke said. 'I need you to help me.'

'Why I wanna do that?' Jackson said.

There was the faint hint of an accent in Jackson's voice. Maybe Caribbean, Burke thought.

'Couple nights ago,' Burke said, 'Paglia sent two guys to kill Jackie, in his home, while his wife was there.'

'Paglia's a pig,' Jackson said. 'Got no style.'

'How come he's able to do business up here?' Burke said.

'Had a piece of it before I moved in,' Jackson said. 'Seemed easier to let him keep it than take it away from him.'

'Could you?' Burke said.

'Take it away from him? I think we could. What you think, Ellis?'

''Course we could,' Ellis said.

'So that's our leverage,' Burke said.

Jackson smiled.

'Our leverage,' he said. 'I like your style, white boy.'

'I want you to call Paglia off of Jackie.'

'Why I wanna do that?' Jackson said again.

'You and he are the same color,' Burke said.

'Sho nuff,' Jackson said. 'And we all like fish fries and watermelon and picking on the old banjo.'

Burke didn't say anything.

'You want more tea?' Jackson said.

Burke nodded.

'Ellis?' Jackson said.

Ellis poured more tea.

'You like watermelon, Ellis?' Jackson said.

'I do,' Ellis said with no expression, 'and I likes to dance and do the buck and wing.'

Still Burke was silent.

'You can't handle this yourself, Burke?'

'No. Paglia's got, what, fifty people? Sooner or later one of them will get by me.'

The room was quiet. Jackson gestured toward Ellis with his empty glass and Ellis poured him more tea. Burke drank his. Jackson drank his. Ellis stood by the door.

'What you think, Ellis?' Jackson said after a while.

'Jackie's a good player,' Ellis said. 'I like to watch him.'

Jackson drank some more tea.

'I do too,' he said.

Burke sat silently.

'I'll have Ellis speak to Johnny,' Jackson said. 'That doesn't end it, let me know.'

'It'll end it,' Ellis said.

33

The St. Albans section of Queens was for Negroes with some money. The houses were mostly English Tudor set behind small neat lawns which fronted on clean streets. Burke drove Jackie to one of them.

'Walt Sewell,' Jackie said. 'Works for the *Amsterdam News*. It's his kid's birthday.'

'How old?'

'Sixteen.'

'And you're the surprise package?' Burke said.

'Supposed to be. Some people may be surprised to see you.'

'Wrong color?' Burke said.

'Un huh.'

'Anyone know why I'm with you?'

'Nope.'

'Long as they don't lynch me,' Burke said.

Jackie smiled and rang the doorbell. An attractive colored woman came to the door wearing a flowered dress with big puffy shoulders. There was a white flower tucked in her hair. She smiled widely at Jackie.

'I'm Jack Robinson, ma'am...'

'For heaven's sake,' she said, 'I know who you are. Everybody knows who you are. I'm Joan Sewell.'

Her eyes shifted to Burke and showed nothing.

'This is my friend,' Robinson said. 'Mr Burke.'

'Glad to meet you, Mr Burke,' she said. 'Please, come in.'

The room was filled in the center with a buffet table on which there was ham and chicken and roast beef and potato salad and coleslaw and sandwich rolls and a large bowl of pink punch. The people around the table were adolescent girls and boys. Several adults stood in a small group away from the table. One of them came toward Robinson and Burke as they entered.

'Jackie,' he said. 'Thank you for coming.'

He didn't make eye contact with Burke.

'Glad I could make it, Walt. This is my friend Burke.'

Walt put out a hand. Burke shook it.

'Nice to meet you, Mr Burke. You with the Dodgers?'

'Yes, I am,' Burke said.

The kids gathered at the buffet tried not to stare, but all of them looked covertly at Robinson. He went to them and shook hands carefully, one at a time, speaking to each of them, pausing longest with the birthday boy. He had brought an autographed baseball.

'There's punch for the kids,' Walt Sewell said to Burke. 'But something a lot harder for the grownups.'

'How else you gonna get through it?' Burke said.

'Brother, you got that right,' Walt said. 'Care for a taste?'

'Sure,' Burke said. 'Whatever you got.'

'Scotch all right?'

'Sure.'

Jackie was apparently talking hitting with the birthday boy and two friends. With an imaginary bat, he was showing them the grip, with the bat handle up into the fingers, not back in the palm.

'Known Jack long?' Walt said.

'Not so long, but quite well,' Burke said and took a drink of scotch.

The room had beige wallpaper with a darker brown vertical stripe. The wall-to-wall carpeting was caramel-colored. The furniture was white and graceful, with none of the thick mahogany heft that Burke was used to in the furnished apartments of his past. There were French doors at the back of the room that let in a lot of light and appeared to open onto some sort of patio.

'Nice house,' Burke said.

'Thanks,' Walt said. 'It's all Joan. My only contribution is to pay for it.'

He put his arm around Joan's shoulder and she slipped her arm around his waist. Joan's hair was smooth, and bobbed. Her makeup was good.

'Probably worth the money,' Burke said.

They were there for an hour. Everyone was trying to act at ease about Robinson being there. No one seemed to pay much attention to Burke being there. Chocolate cake appeared. And ice cream. Burke declined. He had a second drink instead. When they left, Joan gave each of them a piece of cake wrapped in a napkin.

In the car Burke said to Robinson, 'You want this cake? It doesn't go good with scotch.'

'I'll take it home,' Jackie said. 'Give it to Rachel.'

'Pretty much like any other birthday party I've seen,' Burke said.

'You seen many?'

'Mostly in the movies,' Burke said.

'Where they was white.'

' 'Cept for the butler.'

Robinson smiled.

'What kind of party you think we might have?' Robinson said.

Burke shrugged.

'You white folks either think we dancing around in leopard skin skivvies,' Jackie said. 'Or we sitting around talking how mean all the white folks is to us.'

"Nobody knows the trouble I seen..." Burke sang.

'Yeah. That's sort of it,' Jackie said. 'Actually what we do is eat, and drink, and talk about the kids, and how they doing in school and who oughta be president and how taxes are looking, and did you hear Jack Benny last night? Sometimes, we ain't married, we flirt a little, and try to get laid, if we can.'

Jackie smiled a little.

'Some folks,' he said, 'even if they are married.'

'Sounds pretty USA to me,' Burke said.

'It seems to,' Jackie said.

'So why is it that everybody is bullshit about you playing with the white guys?' Burke said.

'Damned if I know,' Jackie said.

34

Burke was in his usual spot at Ebbets Field. In a box just at the other end of the dugout, Lauren Roach sat with Louis Boucicault and three other men. Lauren and Louis were drinking something from a flask which they passed back and forth. Lauren looked over at him. Burke nodded. Lauren looked away. She put her face next to Louis and whispered something. They both giggled. The flask went back and forth between them. Burke looked at the men sitting in the row behind them. Three, Burke thought, his father has upped the guard detail. Lauren glanced over again at Burke. Her face looked flushed. Boucicault took her face in his hand and turned it back toward him, away from Burke. He held it that way for a moment, staring into her eyes. Then he gave her a long kiss. She responded to it visibly, her body arching forward, her arms around Boucicault. From where he sat Burke could see that her skirt was up over her thighs. He knew she was drunk. When the kiss ended they sat for a time watching the game, her head against his chest, his arm around her shoulders. Boucicault took a long pull at the flask, and, without looking back, handed it over his shoulder, apparently empty, to the man behind him who slipped it into his coat pocket and replaced it with another flask, apparently full.

Burke snapped a wooden match with his thumb and lit a cigarette. He inhaled deeply while he carefully broke the match in two and dropped it on the concrete beneath his seat. The Dodgers were playing the Cardinals, and, with the game tied and the bases loaded, and two men out, Stan Musial doubled off the right field screen. Everyone was on their feet. Dixie Walker's throw was pointless, Jackie cut it off at the pitcher's mound, and all three runners scored. *Stan the Man*, Burke thought.

When Burke looked back at Lauren she was kissing Boucicault again. Boucicault's back was to Burke and Burke could see Lauren's eyes over Boucicault's shoulder. They were wide open. And looking at Burke. He looked back without expression. They held the look. Burke took a long drag on his cigarette and dropped it and stepped on it and let the smoke out slowly so that it drifted up in front of his face. Boucicault broke off the kiss and turned with his arm still around Lauren's waist and looked at Burke. Burke lit another cigarette. Boucicault grinned at him. Burke inhaled more smoke. His face didn't move. Someone yelled, 'Down in front.' Boucicault paid no attention. One of the men with him turned and looked back at the shouter. On the field some of the players were looking into the stands.

'Hey, Burke,' Boucicault said loudly.

Burke said nothing. Boucicault turned Lauren so that she faced Burke in the small standing space in front of the seats. Boucicault put his left hand between Lauren's legs and held her crotch.

'This is mine,' he said.

Lauren leaned against Boucicault as if she enjoyed the display. One of the men seated behind Boucicault leaned forward and said something to him. Boucicault pushed him back into his seat with his free hand. And stood with his hand on Lauren's crotch and stared at Burke.

'You got anything to say, Burke?'

Burke continued to smoke, his gaze on Lauren. Her face was more flushed than it had been. Her skirt was gathered clumsily where Boucicault's hand pressed between her legs. She turned and pushed herself in against Boucicault and kissed him again. Boucicault put both hands on her backside. Several people were now yelling for them to sit down, and a number of other people were whistling as they kissed. They held the kiss for a long time, then they broke and Boucicault took her wrist and led her up the aisle, with the three men behind them. Lauren took a long pull on the flask as they left.

Burke watched them go, then he sniped out the cigarette and turned his attention back to the game.

Bobby

Sex was shameful and corrupt. All of us knew it, especially the Catholic kids, who knew it was cause for eternal damnation. And those fires of hell were far more convincing to us than the joys of salvation. We knew that VD was lurking. We knew that pregnancy was nearly unavoidable. The girls knew that if they did it no one would marry them. I knew that my mother would never speak to me again.

These were dire consequences, and we all knew them. But the great unspoken certainty was that any of us, given the chance, would have risked everything for a moment's penetration. We knew that dirty pictures endangered our souls. But if someone had one we would rush to look. We knew that masturbation was evil. But were not dissuaded. We knew people did it. The movies even hinted at it sometimes. 'Howard Hughes presents Jane Russell in The Outlaw.' Every once in a while my parents, especially after cocktails, would be sort of huggy, as if they were more than friends who loved each other and had a son.

The culture presented premenopausal women to us as girls. In the movies married men and girls slept in separate beds. In the movies men would fight for these girls, die for their girls. In the movies girls would scream for their men, tremble for them, dress their wounds, cry for them, wait for them. Love was everywhere. Passion was everywhere. Devotion was everywhere. Self-sacrifice abounded. Sex was nowhere. Except that the girls were sexy. And they were everywhere, on the radio, in the movies, in the magazines, in the ads. The songs. 'To spend one night with you, in our own rendezvous.' The lingerie ads, bathing suit ads, stocking ads, car ads, canned ham ads, beer ads, hair tonic ads, aftershave ads. All of them fresh and clean and sweet and perky and crucifyingly desirable.

In that time we were taught by women, managed by women, admonished by women, brought up by women, punished by women, all through our adolescence. Writhing in the great unacknowledged polarity between culture and biology. Yearning to get laid. Fearing for our souls.

Marriage was our hope. The happiest condition. Loving wife. Children. Contentment. Better to marry than burn.

35

It was nearly midnight when Burke walked down Forty-sixth Street and into a bar called Freddy's on Eighth Avenue. It was not very busy. A Negro with a touch like Teddy Wilson was playing piano. Paglia was sitting in a big round booth near the front with Cash. There were three bottles of red wine open on the table, in front of him, and three glasses. Paglia was drinking from one of the glasses. Burke sat down in the booth.

'Trying some new wines,' Paglia said. 'Want some?'

Burke shook his head. He nodded at Cash, who nodded back.

'Want something else?' Paglia said.

'I'll take Vat 69,' Burke said. 'On the rocks.'

Paglia glanced at the bar and a waiter hurried over.

'Give him Vat 69 on the rocks,' Paglia said. 'Make it a double.'

The waiter hurried off.

'You been talking with Wendell Jackson,' Paglia said.

Burke shrugged. The waiter appeared, put Burke's scotch on the table and hurried away.

'This your place?' Burke said.

'Yeah. I got a lotta places.'

Burke nodded and sipped his scotch.

'I been talking with Wendell, too,' Paglia said.

'Everybody's talking,' Burke said aimlessly.

'I do a lot of business in Harlem,' Paglia said.

Burke held his glass up, and looked at the light through the scotch, and took another swallow.

'Me and Wendell get along.'

'Good,' Burke said.

'Need to get along with Wendell if you do business in Harlem.'

'I heard that,' Burke said.

Paglia poured some wine and drank it and poured some more.

'I like Harlem,' Paglia said. 'You can buy stuff cheap and charge high. The jigs got no place else to go.'

The Negro who played like Teddy Wilson was doing variations on 'Don't Get Around Much Anymore.'

Burke listened to the music while he waited.

'Wendell wants a favor from me,' Paglia said.

He drank some more wine.

'He wants me to give Robinson a break.'

'Stick together, don't they?' Burke said.

'Jigaboos? Yeah, I guess they gotta. Anyway, we had a good chat, Wendell's one of the smart ones, and I said I'd talk to you, see what we could work out.'

'White of you,' Burke said.

Cash smiled. Paglia paid no attention.

'So what do you want?' Paglia said.

'Lay off,' Burke said.

'Lay off what?'

'Lay off Robinson,' Burke said. 'No shooters, nothing. Leave him alone.'

'Who told you I was botherin' him?'

'You can probably figure that out,' Burke said.

Paglia stared at him for a time, silently, then poured some more wine, this time from a different bottle, into the same glass.

'That sonova bitch,' Paglia said. 'You shoulda killed him, too.'

'Probably shoulda,' Burke said. 'We got a deal?'

'That boy can play, can't he?' Paglia said.

'Yep.'

'Hell, I'll give him a pass,' Paglia said.

'Spell it out,' Burke said.

Paglia smiled. He was feeling the wine.

'I'll lay off Robinson,' he said. 'No shooters, nothing. I'll leave him alone.'

'Fine,' Burke said.

Paglia smiled some more.

'You're covered by the deal too,' he said. 'Wendell likes you.'

'That's swell,' Burke said. 'I have your word?'

'You got my word, soldier,' Paglia said.

Burke finished his scotch.

'Thanks for the drink,' he said.

Paglia was drinking wine again, nodding his head in time to the piano music.

'Show him out, Cash,' Paglia said.

Cash got up and Burke followed him. They went out onto Eighth Avenue together.

'His word good?' Burke said to Cash.

'No,' Cash said. 'But he'll stick by this. As long as Wendell can squeeze him out of Harlem, if he don't. It would cost him too much money.'

'So I can trust the money,' Burke said.

Cash grinned.

'You can always trust the money,' he said.

36

There were always people hanging around the players' exit at every ballpark, many of them women. They were there when Burke and Jackie came out of Ebbets Field after a night game with the Pirates. A number of the women were Negroes, and they shrieked and giggled like bobby soxers as Jackie walked past. Burke always disliked these moments. Some women reached out toward Robinson, trying to touch him. Burke always tried to keep himself between Jackie and everyone else. No one paid him any attention. He was an invisible man in the glare of Jackie's visibility.

Some of the women offered themselves.

'You come on down to my house, Jackie... You want some lovin', Jackie, you come right here to me... You looking for a home run, honey... Jackie, you get your sweet self over here to momma...'

A lot of men and boys pushed things at Jackie to sign. Some tried to shake his hand. Some tried to talk with him.

'That Kirby Higbe ain't got no chance with you, Jackie...

Dixie Howell can't never throw you out… We with you, Jackie, we with you…'

As they moved through the crowd a light-skinned, well-built Negro man in a good suit, wearing sunglasses, stepped in front of them.

'Evenin', Mr Burke,' he said. 'Mr Robinson.'

Burke said, 'Ellis.'

'Wendell want to know everything working out copacetic with Mr Paglia.'

'Fine,' Burke said.

Jackie looked at Burke and back at Ellis.

'Excellent,' Ellis said. 'Wendell say in that case he like to meet Mr Robinson.'

'Who's Wendell?' Jackie said.

'Wendell Jackson,' Ellis said. 'He done you a big favor. Your boy here ain't telling you?'

Jackie looked at Burke. Burke shook his head.

'Guess he didn't,' Jackie said. 'What's the favor?'

'Took Gennaro Paglia off your back.'

'Tell him thanks,' Jackie said.

'You don't seem to get the idea,' Ellis said. 'Wendell Jackson wants to meet you, you say where and for how long. Dig?'

Jackie looked at Burke.

'Whaddya think?' he said.

'He did us a favor,' Burke said. 'Easiest thing is to meet him and say thank you.'

Ellis nodded toward the street.

'This way,' Ellis said.

'Sure,' Jackie said.

He and Burke walked behind Ellis to the street where a black four-door Chrysler sedan was parked at the curb. Ellis opened the back door. Burke got in first and Robinson followed. Ellis closed the door behind them and leaned on the car fender again. In front there was a thick-necked black driver, who didn't turn around, and Wendell Jackson, who did. He sat sideways and rested his left arm on the seat back.

'I'm Wendell,' he said.

'Nice to meet you,' Jackie said. 'Understand you did me a favor.'

'Understand?' Wendell said. 'He didn't tell you?'

'Burke don't talk much,' Jackie said.

The street was empty now. Two cops who had been on duty outside the park headed for their squad car, parked across the street. They paused and looked at Wendell's Chrysler, with Ellis leaning on the fender. One cop went on to stand beside his car, the other one took his nightstick out and walked across the street slapping the nightstick gently against his thigh. He had a round face and very small eyes.

Burke heard Ellis say, 'Evenin', Officer.'

'What are you doing here, boy?' the cop said. 'You looking for trouble?'

Ellis murmured something Burke couldn't hear and stepped away from the car. The officer stepped away with him.

'I do,' Wendell said. 'I like to talk.'

Jackie nodded.

'While ago,' Wendell said, 'you embarrassed Gennaro Paglia in one of his joints uptown.'

'Didn't set out to,' Jackie said.

'No, don't suppose you did. But Paglia pushed you kinda hard and you pushed back and White Hope Burke here, he pushed back too, and Gennaro got kind of showed up in his own joint. He don't like to be embarrassed.'

'Most people don't,' Jackie said.

'Gennaro don't like it even more if he gets embarrassed by colored folks.'

Robinson was silent.

Outside the car, the cop said to Ellis, 'Okay, just watch your step. You're in Brooklyn now, boy, you ain't struttin' with some high yellow on Lenox Ave.'

'Yassah, Officer,' Ellis said.

As the cop walked back to his partner, he put the night-stick away and folded something and put it in his pocket.

'So he's out to even it up,' Wendell said, 'and Burke he come to me and say can I maybe do something to calm Gennaro down, and I say, sho'. And Ellis goes and talks with Gennaro and we, ah, reach a meetin' of the minds.'

'Which was to take him off my back,' Jackie said.

'Exactly,' Wendell said.

Across the street the police car pulled away. Outside Wendell's car Ellis was leaning on the fender again whistling softly to himself. Burke thought it might be 'Sing, Sing, Sing.'

'Thanks,' Robinson said.

'You welcome,' Wendell said. 'You didn't tell him none of this, Burke?'

'I don't talk much,' Burke said.

'You sure don't,' Wendell said. 'Anyway, I done you a favor, Jackie, and I hopin' maybe you might do me one, sort of even us up.'

'What do you want?' Jackie said.

'Well, I seen some games this year. And I see you playing out of position.'

'Got Stanky at second,' Jackie said. 'Need a first baseman.'

'Sure,' Wendell said. 'That's right. But still means you sort of new. Make some mistakes.'

Jackie nodded.

'Everybody understands that,' Wendell said. 'Even if the mistake cost a game sometime. Hell, especially with a low-ball pitcher, first baseman involved in half the plays in the game.'

Jackie nodded again. Burke saw where this was going. He suspected Jackie did too.

'You make the right mistake at the right time, game go either way,' Wendell said.

'You going to tell me when the right time is?' Jackie said.

'Yes, I am,' Wendell said.

'Can't do that,' Jackie said.

'Why not?'

'Ain't gonna give you a lecture,' Jackie said. 'Appreciate what you did for me with Paglia, but I can't do you that favor.'

'What are we going to do with this boy, Burke?' Wendell said.

'Watch him play. Clap when he gets a hit.'

No one in the car said anything else. The driver continued to be perfectly still. Burke could see the stress of his shoulders on the back of his coat. Wendell stared at the two men in the back seat.

'So,' Wendell said after a while, 'what's a big old cracker like you doing hanging 'round with this nigger boy?'

'They pay me to,' Burke said.

Wendell looked at both of them some more. Then he raised his voice.

'Ellis?'

Ellis opened the back door and held it. Burke nudged Robinson and he climbed out. Burke climbed out after him. Ellis stood looking into the front seat at Wendell.

'Get in the car, Ellis,' Wendell said.

Ellis smiled. He nodded at Burke and Robinson and climbed into the back seat.

Through the open window in the front Wendell looked out at Burke.

'You understand why he can't tank me a couple games?' Wendell said.

Burke didn't answer right away.

But finally he said, 'Yeah. I understand that.'

Wendell shook his head. The Chrysler started up.

'Deal still hold?' Burke said.

Wendell looked out the window at the two men on the late-night sidewalk.

'For the moment,' he said.

And the Chrysler pulled away.

Box Score 8

Pittsburgh.	AB.	H.	O.	A.	Brooklyn.	AB.	H.	O.	A.
Rikard, rf	4	2	4	0	Miksis, 2b	4	2	0	1
Russell, cf	4	1	1	0	Robinson, 1b	4	1	10	1
Gustine, 3b	4	1	1	0	Reiser, cf	4	1	2	0
Kiner, lf	2	0	3	0	Vaughan, 3b	4	0	0	3
Greenberg, 1b	4	0	6	1	Walker, rf	4	1	4	0
Cox, ss	4	1	0	3	Hermanski, lf	3	1	1	0
Bloodworth, 2b	4	0	4	3	Edwards, c	3	1	8	0
Kluttz, c	3	0	5	0	Rojek, ss	3	1	1	1
Howell, c	1	0	0	0	Branca, p	3	0	1	2
Bonham, p	2	0	0	1	Casey, p	1	0	0	0
*Salkeld	1	1	0	0					
Singleton, p	0	0	0	0					
					Totals	33	8	27	8
Totals	33	6	24	8					

```
Pittsburgh .................0 0 0   0 0 0   0 1 0—1
Brooklyn ..................0 1 0   1 0 0   1 0 *—3
```

*Batted for Bonham in eighth. R—Salkeld, Miksis, Walker, Hermanski. E—Cox. RBI—Rojek, Edwards, Miksis, Russell. 2B—Walker. Hermanski. Edwards. 3B—Robinson. HR—Miksis. SB—Walker, Hermanski. BB—Bonham 1, Singleton 2, Branca 2. SO—Bonham 5, Branca 4, Casey 2. Hits—Bonham 8 in 7, Branca 5 in 7 1-3. Winner—Branca. Loser—Bonham. Umpires—Henline, Stewart and Magerkurth. Attendance—33,207.

37

The day game with Pittsburgh was rained out, and Burke drove Jackie uptown to a meeting. The wipers moved steadily. There was something sort of cozy, Burke thought, about a car in the rain. Sort of safe.

In the meeting room there was the same coziness, lights on during the day, rain sheeting down the windows evenly. There was a large table in the middle of the room and six black men seated around it. There were drinking glasses at each place and a large pitcher of ice water on the table. There was one empty chair. Robinson introduced Burke. Everyone was polite.

A white-haired Negro man gestured Jackie toward the empty chair at the table.

'Sit down, Jackie,' he said. 'Sit down, please.'

Jackie sat. Burke found a chair against the wall near the door and sat in it. Everyone was quiet. Jackie waited.

'Jackie,' the white-haired Negro said, 'perhaps you could ask your friend to wait outside for us?'

Jackie shook his head.

'What we have to say, Jackie, is really rather confidential.'

'He stays,' Jackie said.

'We are not comfortable with that,' the white-haired Negro said.

Jackie leaned forward at the table. Burke sat on his chair by the door as if they were talking of someone else.

'Why is that?' Jackie said.

The white-haired man didn't speak for a moment. He looked at the other men around the table.

'He's not one of us,' the white-haired man said.

Jackie nodded slowly, his hands clasped before him at the table.

'I have trusted him with my life for the last four months,' he said. 'You gonna have to trust him for an hour. Or both of us leave.'

One of the other men at the table spoke.

'Okay, Bascomb,' he said. 'Let it go.'

He was a big muscular man who had gotten fat. His nose had been broken. There were scars around his eyes, and his hands looked thicker than they should have, and a little misshapen. He looked steadily at Burke as he spoke. His black oval eyes didn't blink. Burke looked back.

'Bascomb's a lawyer,' the big man said. 'He can't help himself.'

Burke shrugged.

'You used to fight,' the big man said.

'You, too,' Burke said.

'You win? the big man said.

'Some,' Burke said.

'But not enough to keep doing it.'

'No,' Burke said.

'Me either,' the big man said.

He turned back to Jackie.

'You know everybody in this room,' the big man said. 'Hell, you played for a couple of them.'

Jackie nodded.

'We gave you a chance to play,' the big man said, 'and treated you as good as we could.'

'Probably did, Maurice,' Jackie said. 'Doesn't mean it was good.'

'I know,' Maurice said. 'Money's hard and it's harder if you're a black man.'

Jackie didn't say anything. The other men at the table were motionless. The rain was steady against the windows. Burke was silent beside the door.

'Here's the situation,' Maurice said. 'You stay in the white leagues and pretty soon some other boys be following you.'

Jackie nodded.

'And pretty soon all the teams, St. Louis, everybody, be getting Negro players,' Maurice said, 'and we won't have no players that matter, and the fans won't come, and the Negro leagues are gone.'

Jackie nodded.

'You unnerstand that?' Maurice said.

'I do.'

'That's gonna come no matter what anyone says now.'

'I think that, too,' Jackie said.

'So what happens,' Maurice said. 'Not just to us, but to all the players – the ones that ain't good enough, or be too old now. Where they gonna play?'

Jackie shook his head.

'You don't know,' Maurice said. 'And we don't know either.'

'I can't stop that happening,' Jackie said.

'We think you can,' Maurice said. 'Tell him, Bascomb.'

The white-haired man cleared his throat twice.

'You know, Jackie, how much DiMaggio is making?'

'Yes.'

'You could make that much.'

'Maybe I will,' Jackie said.

'We prepared to pool our money, all the owners, and pay you what they pay DiMaggio, if you'll play for any team in the Negro leagues.'

'Any team?'

'Don't matter which.'

'And I don't play for the Dodgers anymore?'

'No.'

'DiMaggio's making eight times what I make,' Jackie said.

'You be worth it,' Bascomb said. 'And you save the leagues. Give jobs to a lotta colored players.'

Jackie sat back in his chair and unfolded his hands and put them flat on the tabletop. He looked at the men gathered at the table. Then he looked at Burke. Burke didn't move. Jackie looked back around the table again.

'I can't do that,' he said.

'You mean you won't,' Bascomb said.

'Whatever you like,' Jackie said.

'We could probably up the ante,' Bascomb said.

'No,' Jackie said.

'You unnerstand,' Maurice said, 'what it would mean to a lot of colored folks?'

'What I'm doing now means something.'

'Maybe what we're asking would mean more,' Maurice said.

'No,' Jackie said. 'It wouldn't.'

38

It was still raining as Burke drove downtown. The taillights of the cars were like jewels in the rain. Jackie sat beside Burke staring through the front windshield where the wipers moved back and forth. His hands were clenched and he began to tap his thighs with them. The tapping got hard.

'Lotta money,' Burke said.

'Everybody wants a piece,' Jackie said as if Burke hadn't said anything. 'Everybody wants a damn piece.'

'Nothing new there,' Burke said.

'I know.'

'Take it as a compliment,' Burke said.

'Thing is what they say make some sense,' Jackie said. 'Be other colored players coming along after me, and eventually all the good ones be playing in the white leagues.'

'Ain't that sort of the idea?' Burke said.

'Be putting a lotta Negroes out of business,' Jackie said. 'The Negro leagues go under, and a lot of Negro players, the ones with less skill, gonna be out of a job.'

'True for white players too,' Burke said.

'White?' Jackie said.

'Every Negro comes into the major leagues,' Burke said, 'is one less white man.'

Jackie was silent for a moment as they drove downtown in the rain.

'Hadn't thought of that,' he said after a while.

'Nothing's simple,' Burke said. 'You're doing a good thing.'

Jackie looked at Burke in silence for almost a full block.

Then he said, 'Burke, you been thinking about this. I didn't know you thought about anything.'

'I got nothing else to do,' Burke said.

'So what else do you think?'

'Don't you read *Time* magazine? You're conducting a fucking social experiment.'

Jackie nodded.

'And when it's over,' Burke said, 'five years down the line, ten, whenever, the best players are the ones gonna make the show. Spics, spades, Yids, A-rabs, Eskimos, Japs, fat guys from Baltimore, whoever can make it, makes it.'

Jackie didn't say anything. Burke didn't say anything else. The city glistened as they drove through it. The rain-washed cabs were clean yellow. The traffic lights blurred by the rain looked like wet flowers. Every lighted window along the street looked cozy behind the steady gray rain slant. Restaurants looked inviting. The streets were shiny black. The people on the streets and in the doorways, collars up, umbrellas opened, looked peaceful. A policeman in a gleaming slicker and hat was directing traffic around a street excavation. Burke slowed, but the cop waved him forward. And they drove on past.

39

Burke's phone rang in the morning while he was still asleep. He glanced at his wristwatch on the night table as he answered. It was 6:10.

Burke said, 'Hello.'

He could hear breathing at the other end of the phone line, but no one spoke. He fumbled a cigarette from the package beside his watch, and lit it. On an empty stomach it tasted harsh.

'Hello?' he said.

Breathing.

'I'll give it one more hello,' Burke said.

'It's me,' a voice said.

Burke knew the voice.

'Lauren,' he said.

'Yes. I just got home.'

'Un huh.'

'He's going to kill Robinson,' she said.

'Who is?'

'Louis.'

'Why?'

'I don't know. If he knew I told you he'd kill me.'

'When?' Burke said.

'Sunday, during the doubleheader against Pittsburgh.'

'At Ebbets Field?' Burke said.

'Yes.'

'Tell me what you know,' Burke said.

'You can't ever tell him I told,' she said.

'I won't. Tell me what you know.'

'I don't know anything else.'

'He told you he was going to kill Jackie,' Burke said. 'Tell me about that.'

'Yes,' Lauren said. She seemed to be having trouble breathing.

'Okay,' she said. 'Okay... we were drunk and crazy with pills and he said did I ever think about you... and I said no... which was a lie... and he said how about when we were doing it, you know, sex, did I ever pretend he was you... and I said no... And he said he didn't believe me... And he laughed and said here's something to get your attention... He said, I'm going to kill Jackie Robinson... And I said how about Burke, are you going to kill Burke... And he kind of laughed and said *I'm* not going to... As if maybe, you know, somebody else was.'

'Is it to get even with me?'

'I don't know.'

'If that's it, why not kill me?'

'His father. His father told him to stay away from you.'

'And he does what his father says?'

'If he says it... if he says it in a certain way... Louis is afraid of him.'

'Is he going to do it himself?'

Lauren laughed. Burke thought it sounded ugly.

'Of course not… He'll have it done… He'll want to watch… and giggle.'

'Do you know who will do it?'

'No. He has lots of people.'

'Can you find out any more?'

'No. God no. No. He'd kill me in an awful way if he knew I even called you.'

'I've got to tell the cops.'

'No. You can't. He'd know. Please, please, please. You can't.'

'Jesus Christ,' Burke said.

'My God, I hear him coming. Please!'

She hung up. Burke sat on the bed holding the phone for a time and then very slowly, as if it were difficult to do, he carefully placed the phone back in its cradle. He sat some more. The light outside his window got a lighter gray. From the bedside table, he picked up the big GI .45 which was his legacy of the war and looked at it for a moment. Then, holding it, he stood, and walked to the window, and looked down at the street, and watched the morning brighten.

40

'We can't ignore the threat,' Rickey said.

'I know.'

'We also can't have Jack playing baseball in an armed camp. We are selling baseball, family entertainment; and we are selling him. People aren't going to come watch him play if they think there will be gunfire, for God's sake.'

'Can't have cops showing,' Burke said.

'Perhaps we best not mention it.'

'The ballpark threat, no. But you need to cover his home. The first thing he'll want to know is about protecting Rachel.'

'Perhaps we best not mention it to him.'

'Get somebody to watch out for Rachel,' Burke said.

'I can arrange for that, I believe.'

'Your word?' Burke said.

'You have it.'

'Good,' Burke said. 'They said they'd shoot him during the doubleheader. That implies while he's playing.'

'It would be a dramatic thing to do,' Rickey said.

'It would,' Burke said.

They both sat silently for a moment.

Then Burke said, 'We both know, Mr Rickey, that complete protection isn't possible.'

Rickey nodded.

'I don't want him hurt,' Rickey said.

Burke said, 'It's like the war, Mr Rickey. All you can do is be ready and do what you can. We'll have to tell Robinson.'

'No.'

'I'll tell him,' Burke said.

'Do you think that's wise? He might be more comfortable, not knowing.'

'I'll tell him,' Burke said.

'And if I instruct you not to?' Rickey said.

'I'll tell him,' Burke said.

Rickey, his cigar clamped in his mouth, was studying Burke. His eyes narrowed.

'And if I fire you?'

Burke sat back a little in his chair. His voice was the same voice that he'd had since Rickey met him, flat, without emotion, not very loud.

'You do what you gotta do, Mr Rickey. Fire me. Don't fire me. I'm going to do what I'm gonna do, and I'm in this until it's over.'

Rickey moved the cigar around without taking it from his mouth.

'Why?' he said.

Burke sat for a minute rubbing his palms together, looking at his hands, which were slightly distorted from prize-fighting.

'All my life,' he said flatly, looking at his thickened hands, 'I never done anything amounted to jack shit.'

'You were in the war,' Rickey said. 'That was worth something.'

'That was me and ten thousand other guys going where they sent us, doing what they told us – which was to kill ten thousand Japs who went where they were sent and did what they were told.'

'Many consider you a hero, Burke.'

'I got shot to pieces on Bloody Ridge,' Burke said, ''cause that's where they sent me. And that's what they told me to do.'

'In defense of liberty,' Rickey said.

'Sure,' Burke said. 'Probably was.'

'But it's not enough?'

'Enough?' Burke said. 'It's a fucking Fourth of July speech, for which I got destroyed.'

'But Jackie?'

'Jackie's my chance,' Burke said.

'For what?'

'Not to stay destroyed,' Burke said.

'And he amounts to a lot more than jack shit,' Rickey said.

Burke nodded.

'I think it will be best,' Rickey said, 'if you tell him of the threat.'

'I'll tell him,' Burke said.

'And no one else,' Rickey said. 'It will remain our secret.'

'Sure.'

41

'You could take Sunday off,' Burke said.

'I could,' Jackie said. 'And if I told you I wasn't scared I'd be lying.'

'You been scared since this started,' Burke said.

Jackie looked at him hard.

'You think so?'

'Sure. You're alone against the world and people hate you. Of course you're scared. Nothing wrong with that.'

'I'm not alone,' Jackie said. 'I'm with Rachel.'

'Yeah,' Burke said. 'You are.'

'And I had all those people up on Lenox Avenue when Paglia wanted to shoot me.'

'Yeah,' Burke said. 'You did.'

Jackie grinned suddenly.

'And I got you.'

Burke laughed without amusement.

'Hot dog!' he said. 'You want to take Sunday off?'

'Can't,' Jackie said. 'Then we get a letter saying they gonna kill me on Monday? I take Monday off? Tuesday? Wednesday? The season?'

Burke nodded.

'Okay,' he said. 'I get it.'

'You gotta see to protection for Rachel,' Jackie said.

'I've got Rickey's word,' Burke said. 'There will be people with her.'

Jackie nodded.

'All right,' he said. 'Then we just go about our business.'

'It may be nothing anyway.'

'And if it's something,' Jackie said, 'you'll handle it.'

'Sure,' Burke said.

'So you worry about it,' Jackie said.

'Sure,' Burke said.

42

Burke drove up to Harlem to Wendell Jackson's pool hall.

'I was hoping you'd let me borrow Ellis next Sunday,' Burke said.

'Why?'

'Got a letter says a guy is going to kill Robinson.'

'During a game?'

'Yes.'

'So what you think Ellis gon' do?' Jackson said.

'I figure he can shoot,' Burke said.

Ellis, leaning against the wall by the door, had no expression on his face. Jackson smiled.

'That right, Ellis? Can you shoot?'

'I can shoot,' Ellis said.

'So who you want Ellis to shoot?' Wendell said.

'Anybody tries to kill Robinson.'

'That'd pretty sure be a white boy, wouldn't it?'

'Pretty sure.'

Jackson shook his head.

'We like Jackie, don't we, Ellis?'

Ellis nodded.

'And he wanna come up here, we look after him good,' Wendell said. 'That so, Ellis?'

Ellis nodded again. Burke thought that Wendell sounded much more Negro than he had the last time they talked. It was like he was slipping into a disguise.

'But down there?' Wendell shook his head. 'That be white man's work.'

'Protecting Jackie?'

'You think Ellis go down there shoot some peckerwood ofay, and he get treated like a hero?'

'I think he could get away with it,' Burke said.

'That's 'cause you white,' Wendell said. 'Ellis and me know better. That's white man business down there.'

Burke didn't say anything for a time. Wendell and Ellis were still.

Then Burke said, 'The deal with Paglia still there?'

'Ain't heard that it's not,' Wendell said.

Burke nodded.

'Okay,' he said, and stood and walked out of Wendell's office, and through the hostile pool room to the street where his car was parked, and drove downtown.

He put his car in a midtown lot and walked down Eighth Avenue for three blocks to Freddy's. It was the middle of the afternoon and things were slow. Burke went to the bar and laid a ten on the bar.

'My name's Burke,' he said to the bartender, 'I need to see Cash.'

'Cash?'

'Guy walks around with Mr Paglia,' Burke said. 'I need to see him.'

The bartender looked at the ten for a moment. Then he picked it up, folded it skillfully, and slipped it into his side pocket.

'Whaddya drink?' he said.

'Vat 69,' Burke said. 'Ice.'

The bartender poured him the drink.

'I'll see out back,' he said, 'if anybody knows.'

Burke sipped his drink. There were three college-age kids in a booth drinking beer. He remembered before the war, he'd been working high iron at that age and he'd come to New York on a job. Drinking age was eighteen in New York. He remembered feeling liberated. There was a mirror behind the bar and the liquor bottles were arranged in front of it. Backlit by the reflection, they were prismatic. The daylight seeped in through the big front window and mixed with the colored lights on the jukebox, and the lesser lights in the ceiling. There was a large Miss Rheingold sign on the wall. A middle-aged couple sat at the other end of the bar, drinking Manhattans. She was a little old for him, probably, but he liked the slope of her thigh as she sat on the stool. *I used to like quiet bars in the afternoon,* he thought. *I used to like hamburgers with a slice of red onion. I used to like a lot of things.* The bartender returned and made the couple two more Manhattans, and drew three more beers for the kids, and poured more scotch into Burke's glass. He didn't say anything and neither did Burke. The bright blond waitress brought the beer to the booth. One of the kids said something to her and she shook her finger at him. The kids laughed and so did the waitress.

Cash came in and stood for a moment inside the door, waiting, Burke knew, for his eyes to adjust to the dimness. When he could see well, he walked to the bar and sat beside Burke.

'Shot of CC,' he said to the bartender. 'Water back.'

He turned to look at Burke.

'Got a problem?' he said.

'Guy says he's going to shoot Jackie Robinson,' Burke said.

Cash shrugged.

'What guy?'

'Guy I know,' Burke said.

'He tell you?'

'Somebody knows him told me.'

'You believe him?'

'Yes,' Burke said.

'So?'

'Could this be some game Paglia's playing?' Burke said. 'To get around the Jackson deal?'

'No,' Cash said. 'He has someone shot, I do it.'

'You're sure?'

'It ain't Paglia,' Cash said.

The bartender brought Cash his drink. Cash took half of it in a swallow and chased it with some water.

'Whaddya need from me?' he said.

'I need another shooter,' Burke said.

'Me?' Cash said. 'What the fuck has this got to do with me?'

Burke shrugged.

'Why would I do gun work for you or some jigaboo I don't even know?'

Burke shrugged.

'You think it's real?'

'Got to act like it is,' Burke said.

'Yeah,' Cash said. 'You do.'

They were quiet. One of the kids got up from the booth and used the pay phone. The colors of the booze bottles gleamed behind the bar.

'So why'd you ask me?' Cash said. 'For crissake, Paglia may have me kill you someday.'

'Asked Jackson already, he turned me down.'

'One of his own people,' Cash said.

'You were the only other one I could think of.'

'Okay,' Cash said. 'So you ain't got many friends. What in hell made you think I'd do it?'

'You're like me,' Burke said.

'Like you?'

'Un huh. Same kind of guy.'

'What the hell does that mean?' Cash said.

Burke looked into his drink. He thought the silvery transparent ice cubes looked really nice in the rust-colored scotch. He drank most of it.

'You know what we both are,' Burke said.

He looked at himself and Cash, in the mirror, among the pretty bottles. Two men, older than they'd had time to get, both with the same flat look in their eyes.

'We are what we do,' Burke said. 'There's nothing much else.'

'Except the gun and the balls,' Cash said.

Burke smiled a small joyless smile.

'Except that,' he said.

The bartender brought each of them a fresh drink without being asked. He took away the wet coaster napkins and polished the bar in front of them and put out fresh napkins.

'You think you're as good as me?' Cash said.

'Don't know,' Burke said. 'Don't care.'

Cash smiled.

'Me either,' he said.

They drank some of their whisky. The kids at the table stood and straggled boisterously out.

'You care what happens to this nigger, though,' Cash said.

'I'm being paid to.'

'If someone paid you more, would you walk away?'

'You know it doesn't work that way,' Burke said.

Cash nodded.

'You're right,' he said. 'It don't. Can't.'

They both finished their second drink. Cash gestured at the bartender and he brought them a third.

Burke picked his up and looked at it for a moment.

Then he said to Cash, 'I need you to help me.'

Cash drank some of his drink, washed it back with water.

'Okay,' he said.

160

43

Burke and Cash went under the canopied entrance into Ebbets Field. They stood on the Italian marble floor under the baseball bat chandelier as the crowd moved around them.

'We'll start with the upper deck,' Burke said.

Cash nodded. It was well before game time. The Pirates had warmed up and soon the Dodgers would come out. They moved slowly along the back wall at the top of the upper deck, looking. Burke didn't know exactly what he was looking for. He hoped he would know it when he saw it.

Below him on the field the batting cage was in place, and Dixie Walker was hitting. The pitchers were running in the outfield, except for Ralph Branca, who was scheduled to start. The rest of the team lounged alertly on the field in their immaculate whites with the blue trim. Some infielders were in the outfield. Some outfielders and one of the catchers were in the infield, making behind-the-back catches of pop flies. Making trick throws to first. Bruce Edwards would bounce the ball off his biceps before he threw it. Jackie was apparent where he stood, behind the batting cage, waiting his turn. Burke knew that Walker didn't like playing with Jackie, but from here there was no sign of it.

They moved slowly along, looking at the spectators who had already started to come in. Mostly men, many of them with boys, scorecards already purchased; peanuts, and Coke, beer, and steamed hot dogs already going in.

Jackie got into the cage and began to hit. He always looked as if he would fly apart, Burke thought, when he hit. But the bat always came level when it made contact with the ball. Against the soft tosses of Clyde Sukeforth, it was all line drives. Burke always thought the pregame warmups were probably the kindest part of the game, unpressured in front of only an early scatter of fans, time to see who could spit tobacco the farthest, and check the stands for women, and talk of curve balls, and getting laid, and their favorite thing to drink. Most of them could talk about the war as well, but except for a few GI phrases, as far as Burke could tell, they did not.

They reached the Bedford Avenue end of the upper deck, where the right field screen began, and turned and began to stroll back. Looking at everyone, examining every place a man with a gun might hide. The crowd kept coming. The Dodgers starters were taking the infield: Robinson, Eddie Stanky, Reese, and Spider Jorgenson. They went all the way around the park to the center field stands, where Hilda Chester sat with her cowbell, and turned and started back. It was thirty-five minutes to game time. Red Barber and Connie Desmond were in the radio booth slung beneath the upper and lower decks. The umpires had come out onto the field, the crew chief talking to Burt Shotton at the Dodgers dugout. The Dodger Sym-Phony was parading. They came down to the lower grandstand and began the stroll again. As they went behind home plate, looking at everything, Burke saw Louis Boucicault come in with Lauren and a couple of bodyguards. They took a box seat along the third-base line.

'See the guy down there in the white sport coat?' Burke said. 'With the girl in pink?'

Cash saw him.

'He's involved in this thing.'

Cash nodded.

'No matter what might happen,' Burke said, 'the girl doesn't get hurt.'

Cash stared at him for a moment without comment. Then down at Lauren.

'Nice-looking head,' he said.

They moved on.

'If you were going to do it,' Burke said, 'how would you do it?'

They stopped. Cash looked slowly around the field.

'This ain't some freako killing, guy doesn't care if he's caught?'

'No.'

'Gotta be close,' Cash said. 'Otherwise you got to smuggle a rifle in here. Good chance of getting caught.'

'So it's a handgun.'

'Yeah. Which means down close to the field.'

'When he's running in toward the dugout,' Burke said.

'Yes,' Cash said.

'So first-base line, behind the dugout?'

'Yes.'

They were silent.

'And I ain't willing to sacrifice myself to do this,' Cash said.

'No.'

'So I gotta think I can get away with it.'

'Silencer?' Burke said.

'I would,' Cash said. 'Wait until he's coming to the dugout, and everybody's on their feet cheering, and when he reaches the dugout, he's, what, eight feet away, maybe? Pop! Put the gun on the floor, turn around, walk out. Ten, fifteen steps and you're in among the crowd and nobody knows who you are.'

'So we're looking behind the dugout?'

Cash nodded.

'Guy, probably first row of boxes,' he said. 'Dressed so he can conceal a handgun. Maybe with a silencer.'

'Or carrying the gun in a bag,' Burke said. 'Like he brought his lunch.'

'He's got a silencer, it's pretty sure to be an automatic,' Cash said.

Burke nodded.

'Which means he got a couple extra rounds,' he said.

'Good to keep in mind.'

The field was cleared. The umpires were gathered at home plate. Billy Herman came out of the Pirates dugout with his lineup card. Clyde Sukeforth brought the lineups out for the Dodgers. Cash and Burke went to stand in the aisle behind the Dodgers dugout. Burke stayed shadowed in the runway.

'Don't want the guy I pointed out to see me,' Burke said.

Cash shrugged.

'We have to shoot,' Burke said, 'I'd just as soon not explain it to the cops.'

'We have to shoot,' Cash said, 'we hotfoot it out of here right after, just like the shooter would have. Be in Coney Island looking at broads, before any cops show up.'

'Okay, nobody in this thing knows you,' Burke said. 'See what you see, behind the dugout.'

Cash moved along the aisle, looking at the people. The Dodgers ran out to the field, Jackie among them, trotting, pigeon-toed, to first. Billy Cox swung the weighted bat outside the batter's box while Vic Lombardi finished his warmups. Cash walked back to the runway.

'Guy right back of the right-hand end of the dugout,' Cash said. 'Short-sleeve Hawaiian shirt,' Cash said. 'Brown paper bag. Eating a sandwich.'

Keeping his back toward the third-base line where Boucicault sat with Lauren, Burke studied the man, before he stepped back into the runway.

'Paper bag's big enough,' Burke said.

Cash nodded.

'And he's at the right end of the dugout,' Cash said. 'Robinson coming in from first.'

'Any other prospects?'

'Half a dozen guys with loose shirts, or sport coats. But I like the Hawaiian shirt. Most people don't bring their lunch to the ballpark. No dogs? No beer? Perfect position?'

Burke nodded. They were quiet.

'Guy in the white coat,' Cash said. 'Got a perfect seat to watch.'

'That would be his style,' Burke said.

'The ball goes up,' Cash said, 'you want me to shoot him, too?'

'Not if you don't have to.'

'Sure.'

'I'll stay here,' Burke said. 'You go down toward right field a way. Something happens we'll have a crossfire going.'

'How about civilians?' Cash said.

'I'm going to keep Jackie alive,' Burke said.

'Even if it costs a couple civilians?'

'If it has to,' Burke said, 'it has to.'

Cash smiled faintly and turned and stepped out of the runway and strolled along the aisle toward right field, to the next runway, and stopped there and leaned on the wall to watch the action.

It came in the fourth inning. With Billy Cox on first and two out, Frank Gustine doubled into the left field corner. Cox stopped at third. The next batter, Ralph Kiner, hit the ball to the deepest part of left-center field. Carl Furillo, playing center, caught the ball with his back to home plate, and banged into the Van Heusen shirt sign and held the ball. Hilda rang her cowbell. The fans stood and cheered and clapped and whistled as Furillo trotted in. Burke stepped out of his concealment in the runway with his gun out and cocked and held behind his right thigh. Jackie came to the bench. Among the rest of the fans applauding Furillo, the man in the Hawaiian shirt took something from his lunch bag and extended his arm. Burke shot him twice in the middle of the back. As he fired, he heard Cash's gun from off to his right. Blood appeared on the man's face. He half turned and fell onto the roof of the Dodgers dugout. Most of the fans didn't notice. Those around him stood frozen for a moment. Burke put his gun away and turned and walked back down the aisle where he'd stood. He walked under the stands and past the concession booths and out through the rotunda, and left onto Sullivan Place. Cash fell in beside him and they walked to the parking lot on Bedford Avenue where Burke had left his car.

44

Burke sat beside Jackie in Rickey's office.

'Killer was a known killer for hire,' Rickey said. 'The police presume it was a case of one criminal shooting another.'

'Fairly close,' Burke said.

'You did a hell of a job, my friend.'

Burke nodded.

'I'm doing more harm than good,' he said.

'Oh?'

'There's a personal thing going on here,' Burke said. 'I'm not protecting Jackie anymore. I'm bringing trouble to him.'

'Do you care to discuss the, ah, personal thing?'

'No.'

Rickey nodded slightly, as if to himself, and took his cigar from his mouth and examined the glowing end for a moment.

'It's a woman,' Jackie said.

'How often that's true,' Rickey said. 'What is it about the woman?'

'That's up to Burke to tell you,' Robinson said.

Burke glanced at him. Even in repose there was a kind of energy charge to Robinson. He was not simply black, he was blue-black, Burke thought, and showed no sign that he wasn't proud of it. Rickey looked at Burke.

'And you, sir?'

'I'm quitting,' Burke said. 'You need to get somebody else.'

'I thought you were in this to the end,' Rickey said.

'This is it,' Burke said. 'The shooting was too far along for me to stop it by quitting. Now there's time.'

'Jack?' Rickey said looking back at Robinson.

'No,' Jackie said. 'I won't work with anyone else.'

'You mean that?' Rickey said.

'Burke knows I do,' Jackie said.

It was true. Burke had never known Robinson to say something he didn't mean. He could feel the force in Robinson, and realized, fully, for the first time, what his passivity in public cost him.

'I'm not preventing trouble,' Burke said. 'I'm causing it.'

'Then we'll deal with it,' Robinson said. 'I started this with you. I'm not finishing it with somebody else.'

'Maybe you'll have to.'

'No,' Robinson said. 'I'll finish it with you. Or I'll finish it alone.'

Robinson looked steadily at Burke. Rickey was quiet, waiting.

It was the morning before a day game. There were peanuts roasting somewhere and the scent of them drifted through the office.

'What about Rachel?' Burke said.

'Rachel would say the same thing.'

'You're sure?'

'I'm sure.'

'How the hell can you be so sure?' Burke said.

Burke had an inarticulate sense that he might be talking about more than the present issue.

'Rachel and I aren't separate people,' Jackie said. 'We are two parts of one thing. She can speak for me. I can speak for her. She feels the same way I do.'

Burke was silent. He rocked very slightly in his chair. *What the hell would that be like? Two parts of one thing?* He and Robinson looked at each other. Then Burke nodded with only the slightest movement of his head.

'I'll stay,' he said.

Robinson said nothing at all. But he nodded too, if possible, an even smaller nod than Burke's.

45

The phone rang in the dark. Burke turned on the light. This time it was 4:00 a.m. Burke was pretty sure who it was.

'Hello,' he said.

'Congratulations,' Lauren said.

'For?'

'Thwarting Louis.'

She had trouble saying thwarting. Burke knew she was drunk again.

'Thanks,' he said.

'Couldn't have without me,' she said.

'I know.'

'You grateful?'

'Sure,' Burke said.

She was silent. He was silent. The emptiness hissed quietly on the phone line.

'How grateful?' Lauren whispered. Her voice sounded hoarse.

'Lauren,' Burke said. 'Why are you calling me up?'

'Remember the Cardinals game?' Lauren said. 'Couple of weeks ago? Me and Louis?'

'You and Louis,' Burke said. 'Almost fucking in public.'

'Did you like that?'

'No.'

There was silence for a time.

'So whyn't you do something?' Lauren said.

'None of my business,' Burke said.

'So cold,' she said.

'You don't like him,' Burke said. 'Walk away.'

'And be with who?' she said.

'Up to you,' he said.

'But not you?'

Burke took in a big lungful of smoke.

'There is not enough of me,' Burke said, the smoke drifting out as he talked, 'for you. I can't give you what you need.'

'How the fuck you know what I need?' she said.

'I guess I don't,' Burke said. 'But I know what I need.'

'What is that, Burke? Just what the fuck do you need?'

'I need to be safe,' he said.

'Safe?'

'Un huh.'

Burke sniped out his cigarette and lit another one.

'Safe from what?' Lauren said.

He thought she was probably drinking as she talked. *Four in the morning.* Burke was silent for a time.

'Safe from what?' she said again.

'I don't know,' Burke said. 'I need to stay inside.'

At the other end of the phone, he could hear her swallow.

'And what about me?' she said. 'I can't live like this.'

'Like what?'

'Burke,' she said, 'I'm getting worse. I let him handle me like that in public. He does it all the time. I let you see him do it. I'm drinking more. I'm drinking now. It's four something in the morning, and I'm drinking gin on the rocks.'

'So stop,' Burke said.

'And drugs,' she said. 'He gives me drugs, and when we have sex he likes to… he degrades me.'

'Get away from him,' Burke said.

'I can't, not without you, I can only stop if I'm with you.'

'Then I become him. Then I'm what you can't live without,' Burke said. 'I don't have that in me.'

'If you'll come and get me,' she said, 'if you'll take me and keep me with you, I'll… I'll go to a psychiatrist. I'll go to a hospital someplace, I can be all right, I know I can.'

Burke was silent.

'Jesus, God,' Lauren said. 'Other people went to the war. They came back. What happened to you? Did the war take all of you?'

'Ex-wife took some,' Burke said carefully, his voice entirely flat.

'Don't you understand? We're connected in an awful way. I need someone to care about me.'

'I know,' Burke said.

'And you need to care about something,' she said.

He didn't speak.

'Burke,' she said in a clotted voice, 'I love you.'

Still he didn't speak. The silence hummed between them over the phone line. Then she hung up. Burke sat hunched naked on the bed with his cigarette in his mouth and his arms across his chest. He was shaking. His face was clammy. He felt sick. In the dead silent room he heard his own voice.

'I love you too,' it said.

46

The train crossed the west branch of the Susquehanna River south of Lock Haven. Burke sat in the aisle seat beside Robinson in the back of a Pullman car on the way to Chicago. The second western swing of the season.

'Bob Chipman's going tomorrow,' Jackie said. 'I see him good.'

Burke nodded, looking past Robinson at the central Pennsylvania landscape.

'You miss your wife on road trips?' Burke said.

'Yes.'

The train slowed as it went through Clearfield. They were behind the town, where the laundry hung and the trash barrels stood. Behind sagging barns with tobacco ads painted on the siding. Tangles of chicken wire. Gray scraps of lumber. Rusted stove parts. Oil drums. A sodden mattress.

'He was really going to shoot me,' Robinson said.

'How's it feel?'

'You got shot at,' Jackie said, 'how did that feel?'

'Scared the shit out of me,' Burke said.

Robinson nodded.

'You scared?' Burke said.

'I been scared since I said I'd do this.'

'You could quit.'

'No,' Robinson said. 'I couldn't.'

'Why?'

'You think I should?' Robinson said.

Burke thought about it for a moment.

'Disappoint a lot of people,' he said.

'You think I don't know that?' Robinson said.

'It wore me down,' Burke said. 'Scared every day.'

Jackie nodded.

'This is more public,' he said. 'More, ah, concentrated. But being a Negro man in America in the twentieth century…'

He shrugged.

'So this is like your life already,' Burke said. 'More of the same.'

'Cranked up a little,' Robinson said.

'You get used to it?'

'No.'

170

The train had left Clearfield behind, and picked up speed again. The card game that had begun at Penn Station was still being played. The same people were playing. Sukeforth, Reese, Gene Hermanski, and Eddie Miksis. Some of the players slept. Shotton, the manager, read a book.

'How about you?' Robinson said. 'You get used to it?'

'Being scared?'

'Un huh.'

'I was scared all the time, every day, it got to seem like the only way there was to be.'

'Yeah,' Robinson said. 'That's the feeling. You still got it?'

'War's over,' Burke said.

'That's not what I asked. I asked you if you still felt scared,' Jackie said.

The train passed a small cluster of brown cows standing near a gate. Waiting for feed.

'I don't feel scared,' Burke said. 'Or much anything else.'

'Bother you to shoot that man?' Robinson said.

'No,' Burke said.

Robinson was silent for a time, then he said, 'Tell me about the girl.'

'What's the girl got to do with anything?' Burke said.

Jackie shrugged. They watched the fields of western Pennsylvania lumber past them. Burke had adjusted to the movement of the train the way he had adjusted to the troop ship. It had come to seem the norm.

'I was her bodyguard,' Burke said. 'Keep her away from a guy named Louis Boucicault. He didn't like it.'

'You and the girl?'

'Yeah. For a while.'

'And?'

'Things got out of hand. I had to shoot a couple of people. I got fired.'

'And the girl?'

'When I left she wanted to come with me.'

'Why didn't she?'

'Her father said no.'

'I seen you work,' Robinson said. 'I wouldn't think that would stop you.'

'Girl's trouble,' Burke said.

'So am I,' Robinson said.

Burke looked at Robinson, but didn't say anything. They were both quiet for a long time, before Robinson spoke again.

'Being scared alone,' he said, 'is worse.'

Burke didn't answer. Robinson had nothing else to say. They sat quietly together as the train crossed into Ohio north of Youngstown.

47

Burke sat with Cash at the bar in Freddy's. It was evening. The piano player was doing a delicate version of 'Shine,' his hands barely touching the keys. The room was full of men in summer straw hats and gray suits having a drink, maybe ten, after work.

'What's on your mind?' Burke said.

Cash stared straight ahead at the mirror behind the bar.

'Paglia wants me to shoot you but not kill you,' Cash said.

Burke looked at him silently and waited.

'That make any sense to you?' Cash said.

'No.'

'I told Paglia that,' Cash said. 'It don't make any sense.'

'What'd he say?'

'Said it had to do with Robinson not getting killed.'

'Paglia?' Burke said.

Cash nodded and turned his gaze away from the bar mirror and looked straight at Burke for the first time.

'I was wrong,' Cash said. 'Paglia was involved in that deal to kill Robinson.'

'With Boucicault?' Burke said.

'Here's how it was supposed to go,' Cash said. 'Boucicault, the kid, wants you dead. But his old man, you know, Frank?'

Burke nodded.

'Frank says no. Says he's made a deal with another guy that leaves you out of it.'

'That would be Julius Roach,' Burke said.

Cash nodded.

'I know who he is,' Cash said. 'And Paglia has had a hard-on ever since he got faced down up on Lenox Avenue by Robinson and a roomful of niggers.'

Burke nodded.

'But he's got a lot of interests uptown,' Cash said. 'And if he kills Robinson, then Wendell Jackson closes him down.'

Burke nodded again.

'So, Paglia and Frank Boucicault move in the same circles and one way or another, young Boucicault and Paglia get together,' Burke said.

'You're starting to see it,' Cash said.

'And they make a deal. Boucicault kills Jackie, and Paglia kills me. Boucicault doesn't get trouble from his father and Paglia doesn't get trouble from Wendell.'

'Yep. And, here's the part I like. Boucicault is pressing Paglia to kill you. He says he made a good faith run at Jackie and Paglia owes him one.'

'So Paglia wants to fulfill the bargain enough to keep Boucicault in the deal,' Burke said.

'But if I kill you,' Cash said, 'then he's got no bargaining chip to make Boucicault try Robinson again.'

'So you give him a little,' Burke said. 'You shoot me, but you don't kill me. You that good?'

'Oh, hell, yes,' Cash said.

'You gonna do it?'

'No.'

Burke nodded.

'Paglia broke the rules.'

'Yeah,' Cash said. 'He did.'

They finished their drinks, and ordered two more. The pianist was playing 'Avalon' with a lot of gentle right hand.

'This has to end,' Burke said.

Cash shrugged.

'You want to help me end it?' Burke said.

'What are we ending?' Cash said.

'Paglia and Robinson, me and Boucicault. Lauren. The whole thing.'

'Lauren?'

'Julius's daughter.'

'Lauren,' Cash said.

'Yeah.'

'What's in it for me?' Cash said.

'Nothing.'

Cash nodded.

'Sounds like a hell of a deal,' he said.

'You in?' Burke said.

Cash drank half of his whisky and sipped water behind it.

'Tell me about Lauren,' he said.

48

Burke waited outside the apartment building, until he saw Julius leave. Then he went in. A Negro maid answered the apartment door.

'Tell Mrs Roach that Mr Burke is here about Lauren.'

'Mrs Roach is rarely home to anyone,' the maid said.

'She'll see me,' Burke said and handed a $100 bill to the maid.

'Of course, sir. If you'll wait here in the living room.'

Burke sat. The vast apartment was oppressively quiet. The maid came back.

'Be our secret?' she said.

'Promise,' Burke said.

'This way.'

Burke followed her into a high-ceilinged room that looked out over the park. The furnishings were white, the voluptuous drapes that bunched on the floor were white. The carpet was white. There was a white marble fireplace in which, Burke suspected, no fire had ever been set. On a chaise near the window, where she could see the park, was a silver-haired woman in a white dressing gown, with a white comforter over her legs. Burke thought she looked beautiful. She was drinking sherry from a small fluted glass. The maid lingered near the door.

'Hello,' she said. 'You're Mr Burke.'

Her voice was tentative.

'Yes,' Burke said.

'You know my daughter,' the woman said.

'I do,' Burke said.

He was close to her now and realized that she wasn't beautiful, though once she might have been.

'Would you like some sherry?' she said.

'No thanks,' he said.

'I hope you'll not mind if I sip mine,' she said.

'Not at all,' he said.

She nodded at a white satin chair near the chaise.

'Please,' she said. 'Sit down. Tell me why you're here.'

She finished her glass and took a bottle from the window-sill and poured it full again.

'It helps with the pain,' she said.

'Are you ill?' Burke said.

'I think so,' she said.

'I'm sorry,' Burke said.

'Life,' she said. 'Life makes one ill sooner or later.'

'It can,' Burke said. 'Can't it?'

'Why did you say you came here?'

'I'm looking for Lauren,' Burke said.

'My daughter.'

'Yes.'

The woman nodded. They were quiet.

'Would you like some sherry?' the woman said.

'No thanks.'

The woman nodded again and drank.

'Do you know where Lauren is?' Burke said.

'My daughter. She grew up into a very beautiful woman, don't you think?'

'Do you know where I can find her?' Burke said.

'She's with her husband.'

'Do you know where they live?' Burke said.

'She lives with him,' the woman said. 'With Louis.'

'Where does Louis live?' Burke said.

The woman drank some more sherry. She gestured vaguely toward the window.

'Out there,' she said.

'Out there?'

'Yes.'

She drank again and refilled her glass. The wine didn't seem to affect her. Burke wished that it would.

'You know I never go out there,' the woman said. 'I can see it from here, and I like it. But I never go out there.'

'Do you know an address for Lauren?' Burke said.

'Do you go out there?' she said.

'Sometimes,' Burke said.

He glanced at the maid standing by the door. The maid gestured to him to join her.

'Excuse me, ma'am,' Burke said.

He stood and walked to the maid. She looked at him in the impervious way Negroes looked at whites.

'She don't know,' the maid said softly. 'She don't know this address.'

'You know?' Burke said.

'How much?'

'I got another C-note,' Burke said.

The maid put her hand out. Burke took out the hundred and gave it to her. She folded it neatly and put it in her apron pocket.

'I write it down for you,' she said.

Burke went back to the woman who had once been beautiful.

'It's been very nice talking to you, ma'am.'

'Oh,' she said. 'Yes. Thanks for coming.'

She put out her hand; Burke took it for a moment. Then he let it go and straightened and left the room. On his way out the maid gave him a slip of paper with an address.

49

The house was in Connecticut in the Litchfield Hills, maybe two hours from New York. Burke sat with Cash in the dark car looking at the sweep of the front lawn. It was raining hard again.

'Big house right there,' Cash said. 'Top of the lawn.'

'No gate,' Burke said.

'Doesn't mean no guards,' Cash said.

'Frank Boucicault will have guards,' Burke said. 'We're looking for the carriage house.'

'The happy couple,' Cash said.

Burke nodded without speaking. With the car engine off, the wipers weren't going, and the rain had streaked the windshield. Burke rolled down his side window enough to see out, squinting against the rain, looking for the carriage house.

'If it was for carriages,' Burke said, 'it would be at the end of the driveway.'

'Want to drive in?' Cash said.

'No,' Burke said, 'too bold. We'll walk.'

'Maybe rain will keep everybody inside,' Cash said.

'Maybe,' Burke said.

Burke rolled up his window and got out of the car. Both men wore raincoats and hats. Burke unlocked the trunk of the car and Cash took out a Thompson. Burke hadn't seen one since Guadalcanal. Sheltered by the trunk lid, Cash put the twenty-round magazine in place, tapped the bottom with his palm to seat it, worked the action once to put a .45 round up into the chamber. He pressed the gun, muzzle down, against his thigh, the skirts of his coat partly protecting the gun from the rain. Burke closed the trunk and the two men started up the driveway in the darkness and the heavy rain. There were lights on in the big house. But no movement. As they reached the top of the low upslope, the drive turned a gradual right behind the house. They followed it, hunched against the hard rain. Ahead, among some trees, barely visible in the murk, was a two-story building with a cupola on top. There was a shapeless blur of light. When they got close they could see it was a seeping through some drawn curtains in a first-floor window. The entry door had been cut into the vertical planking of the big carriage house doors. Burke tried the handle. It was locked. He knocked on the door. A voice sounded inside.

Burke thought it might have said, 'Who is it?'

'Your father,' Burke said, in a low voice he hoped would be hard to identify.

There was a moment and then Burke heard the dead bolt turn. The door opened a ways and Burke hit it with his shoulder. It burst open and caught on the security chain bolt. He pulled back. Cash joined him and they both lunged against it. The chain bolt screws tore out of the doorjamb and the door burst open. Wearing a Chinese silk dressing gown, Louis Boucicault had turned away from the door toward the heavy mahogany sideboard against the right-hand wall. Cash was in first. He put the muzzle of the Thompson up snug under Boucicault's chin.

'Still,' Cash said. 'Really still.'

There was a table in the middle of the room with an ice bucket, some lemons, and a bottle of gin. Wearing a Chinese silk dressing gown that matched Louis's, Lauren sat with a glass in her hand. Everything seemed to have frozen. There was fruit on the table, and some cheese and some sort of pâté and a silver bowl of crackers. Burke closed the door behind him and put his gun away inside his raincoat. He went to the sideboard and opened the top drawer and took out a nickel-plated, pearl-handled .32 caliber revolver.

'Cute,' Burke said and slipped it into his coat pocket.

Then he walked to Boucicault and patted him down. He stepped back and pointed at the empty second chair at the table.

'Sit,' he said.

Frozen with the muzzle of the submachine gun pressing up under his chin, Boucicault shifted his eyes to Cash. Cash grinned at him and moved the muzzle.

'Do what he tells you,' Cash said.

Lauren still had neither moved nor spoken. As time began to move at a more normal speed, Burke realized the radio was on, a big Capehart. They were listening to 'The Life of Reilly.'

Louis sat. He drank some gin. Cash pulled an uncomfortable-looking ladder-back chair from the corner past the side-board, and dragged it near the table, and sat with the tommy gun in his lap.

'How'd you get this far?' Louis said.

He was trying to keep his voice steady.

'Weather's bad,' Burke said. 'Can you call your father up at the house?'

'Yes.'

'Call him. Tell him your situation. Tell him he and I need to talk. Tell him if anything happens you go first.'

Lauren slowly raised her glass and sipped some gin. When she had drunk, she lowered the glass, but she did not put it down.

'You want my father to come down here?'

'Yes.'

'Now?'

'Yes.'

'What if he won't come?'

'You're dead,' Burke said.

Burke was aware of the radio. William Bendix. Laughter. The rain was hard on the windows. Carefully, Louis reached for the phone beside the table. He dialed and spoke into it and hung up.

'He'll be right down,' Louis said.

Burke went to the door and opened it, the rain slanted in onto the polished floor. Cash got up and went to the corner of the room, between the sideboard and the wall, keeping the Thompson pointed at Louis.

'Lauren,' Burke said. 'Go over there on the wall past the window. If anything happens, get on the floor.'

She didn't move. Burke went to the table and put his hand

under her armpit and pulled her up and pushed her against the wall and out of the line of fire. Then he went to the other side of the open door and took out the .45 and stood. The rain coming through the open door had begun to puddle and soak into the rag rug when Frank Boucicault came in. Without looking around him he walked to the table where his son sat and looked down at him. Burke closed the door.

'You got people with you, Frank?'

Boucicault turned slowly to look at him.

'Of course,' he said. 'They're all around this building.'

He looked at Cash.

'Who's this?'

'Man with a submachine gun,' Burke said. 'Things happen, Junior goes first, you go second.'

Frank nodded thoughtfully as if Burke had confirmed his suspicions.

'Whaddya want to talk about?' he said.

'You know your kid's got a deal with Gennaro Paglia?'

Frank looked at Louis.

'I'm a grown man,' Louis said. 'I make deals with who I want.'

'You make one with Gennaro Paglia?' Frank said.

'Ask him,' Louis said. 'He's the one telling the story.'

'You gave Julius Roach your word that the kid wouldn't mess with me.'

'I did.'

'I've heard,' Burke said, 'that your word is good.'

'It is.'

'Paglia gave his word to Wendell Jackson, up in Harlem, that he wouldn't mess with Jackie Robinson.'

'I know Wendell,' Frank said.

'So the deal is that Louis kills Robinson for Paglia, and Paglia kills me for Louis.'

Frank looked at his son.

'That the deal?' he said.

'He's lying,' Louis said. 'He's a lying sack of shit.'

Frank nodded. He looked at Lauren standing flat against the wall in the corner. She was perfectly still, still holding her glass of gin. Her face was blank, and very pale.

'That the deal, Lauren?'

The rush of the outside rain was the only sound in the room. Frank kept his gaze on Lauren. Louis turned to stare at her too. Cash watched the Boucicaults. Burke looked at nothing.

Lauren cleared her throat. In a small voice Lauren said, 'That's what Louis told me.'

Frank nodded. He didn't look at his son.

'So what are you doing here?' he said to Burke.

'I want the girl,' he said. 'And I want the three of us to walk out of here safely.'

'Frank,' Louis said. 'They're lying. Both of them, the sonova bitch is trying –'

'Take her,' Frank said.

'Frank,' Louis said. His voice was higher than it had been. 'You bastard, you can't...'

Frank turned and leaned over the table and pointed at Louis. 'Not a sound,' he said. 'Not one more fucking sound.'

Louis opened his mouth, and met his father's look, and closed it. His face was death white except for the redness that smudged his cheeks. Burke could see that he was breathing very hard. Frank turned and spoke to Burke.

'We need somebody dead,' Frank said, 'we do our own killing.'

'You need any of us dead?' Burke said.

'I don't like you much,' Frank said after a moment. 'And I think she's a fucking whore. But my word is how I do business. Louis will never, ever, bother you again.'

'Or her?' Burke said.

'Or her, or Tommy Gun over there. We'll walk up to your car with you. You can drive away. No one will stop you.'

'Your word?' Burke said.

'My word.'

Burke looked at Cash.

'No harm keeping the gun on him while we walk,' Cash said.

'No,' Burke said. 'Point it somewhere else.'

Cash nodded and let the muzzle of the Thompson drop.

Burke put out his hand toward Lauren. Lauren didn't move.

'Where am I going?' she said, her voice barely carried over the sound of the rainfall.

'With me,' Burke said.

'For how long?'

Burke paused for a moment, then smiled slightly.

'Until death do us part,' he said.

She stared at him a moment, then stepped away from her corner and took his hand. Still seated, Louis was pouring gin into his glass. Burke thought he saw tears. Then Frank opened the door and went out first, and they followed him into the downpour.

50

They lay on the bed together at Burke's apartment, smoking. He had an arm around her. She had her head on his chest. Soaked when they got there, they had both showered. Burke was wearing white boxer shorts. Lauren had on one of his shirts. There had been no sex. She touched one of the bullet scars on his chest.

'Scars are looking better,' she said.

'They calm down eventually,' he said.

'They're really quite faint,' she said.

It was nearly dawn. Through the rain the gray day was beginning to show.

'You okay?' he said.

She nodded. He wasn't looking at her, but he could feel her head move on his chest.

'Why?' she said.

'Why what?'

'Why did you come for me?' she said.

'Seemed right,' Burke said.

'Do you love me?' she said.

Burke took in a lot of smoke and let it out slowly and

watched it twine with the smoke from her cigarette as it rose. She waited.

'Yes,' he said at last.

'How long have you loved me?' she said.

'Long time,' he said.

'So why now?'

'It was time.'

'I need to know,' she said.

Burke took in more smoke and held it in his lungs for a moment before he blew it gently out.

'I don't know if I can tell you,' he said finally. 'I… since… the war…'

Absently he touched the scars on his chest. When he did, she covered his hand with hers.

'I been scared since the war,' he said. 'I got hurt too bad.'

'You didn't seem scared.'

'I was scared of caring about anything.'

'Because you could lose it?'

'Because I could lose it.' Burke said.

'And if nothing mattered, you could lose it or not lose it and it couldn't hurt you.'

'Something like that.'

'Even your life,' Lauren said.

'Yeah.'

'So you didn't care about anything, you wouldn't have to be afraid of anything?'

'I guess.'

'So what changed?' she said.

'It was no way to live,' Burke said.

Neither of them said anything. They lay still listening to the rain.

'I think it had something to do with that colored baseball player.'

'Robinson,' Burke said.

'It did,' Lauren said, 'didn't it?'

Burke put his cigarette out in the ashtray on the nightstand, and shook another one loose, and lit it, and took a drag and lay back with the cigarette still in his mouth.

'Probably,' Burke said.

She didn't speak, but he could feel her head nodding slowly against his chest.

'This will not be easy,' Lauren said after a while.

'I know,' Burke said.

'I've been rich too long with my father's money. I have a problem with alcohol, with drugs, with sex, with men, with my mother, with my father...'

'But not with me,' Burke said.

'I have no money of my own, no place to live.'

'You can live with me,' Burke said.

'I can't bear to go near my father's house. I don't even have clean clothes.'

'We'll get some,' Burke said.

'And,' she said, 'you've been in some kind of emotional hibernation since Guadalcanal.'

'Now I'm not.'

'How can you be sure?'

'Can't.'

'But you're hopeful?' she said.

'I'm willing to work at it,' Burke said.

'We will have to work hard.'

'We can do that,' Burke said.

It was full day outside Burke's window, with the rain steady.

'I love you,' Lauren said.

'Yes.'

'Can you tell me you love me?' Lauren said.

'I already did.'

'Do it again.'

'I love you,' Burke said.

She put her cigarette in the ashtray and left it there still smoking. She turned her face up toward him and put her arms around him.

'I want us to make love,' she said. 'I don't want us to fuck. I want us to make love.'

'Now?' Burke said.

'Right now,' she said. 'And hurry.'

Burke reached across her with his free hand and stubbed out her smoldering cigarette butt. Then he said, 'Sure,' and put his face down to hers. Several times as they made love she gasped, 'Hold on to me. Hold on to me.' He wasn't sure if she was crying.

Bobby

I had gone to New York once before with my father. We took the train down, and stayed at the Commodore, and took the subway to Ebbets Field. This time, just turned fifteen, I went alone.

I was visiting in Lynbrook, and took the Long Island Railroad into Penn Station. I lingered in Penn Station for a while, feeling the size and space. Feeling as if I were at the center of civilization with the throb of great engines animating the space. I smelled it: the steam, the peanuts, the energy. Underneath the vast high ceiling of the central room, I was enclosed and free, and small, and adult, and overwhelmed with confidence. Alone, fifteen, in New York City.

I was visiting alone. I'm not sure my parents ever knew.

I took the subway to Broadway and went downtown, reading the maps. I knew I probably didn't have to come into Manhattan at all. I knew I was going a long way round, but it was the way I remembered going with my father, and my newly evolving self wouldn't let me ask directions. The names of the stations were exciting. I'd heard them on WHN. I read about them in The New York Times: *Astor Place, Bleeker Street, Bowery.* This was New York. I was in its heart.

I can no longer remember how I went. I probably couldn't go there now. Somewhere around Canal Street I changed trains, and somewhere around Prospect Park I got off and followed the crowd. Brooklyn wasn't as tall as New York. But it was no less urban. It was late afternoon, before a night game with the Braves. The people were on the street selling programs and peanuts and hot dogs. And the crowd was already gathering. Fathers and sons. The fathers often wearing felt hats, dressed in suit and tie. The sons often with baseball gloves, often with baseball hats. There were women in the crowd and rarely, little girls. There was also a large mix of Negroes. I stood at the intersection of McKeever Place and Sullivan Place in front of the field. I could see the light towers above the stadium. The name EBBETS FIELD in white lettering built into the front at the top. The arches, the Palladian windows, the brick façade, the awning-striped canopy over the entrance. I went into the rotunda and bought my ticket and walked up the stairs and out into the interior grass, red clay infield, blue sky above, some white clouds, the players in their uniforms. The Dodgers in home white, blue lettering, blue hats; the Braves in road gray, red lettering, navy hats with red bills, on their chests a tomahawk.

I bought some peanuts and a program and found my seat on the third-base side. I watched batting practice. I watched infield practice, and the long lazy fungoes being hit to the outfielders. I watched some of the players run sprints in the outfield, and as the sky darkened and the lights took hold, I watched the two pitchers go to the bullpens and begin their warmups. Ralph Branca for the Dodgers. Warren Spahn for the Braves.

I was sitting among Negroes, between two heavy black women. I was alone, a slender white boy too young to shave. They asked me where I was from. I said Boston. They asked me what I was doing there. I said I was a Dodgers fan and wanted to see Jackie. One of the women announced this loudly to the group.

'This boy done come all the way from Boston to see our Jackie.'

She made Boston a long word. Everyone applauded. Some cheered. I imagined that Red Barber, high up in the catbird's seat, might notice and remark that they're tearing up the pea patch over there in the stands behind third. The world exfoliated around me. The Dodger Sym-Phony was marching back and forth. Hilda Chester was ringing her cowbell. Eddie Bataan was blowing his whistle. I was here, unaccompanied, unsupervised, alone, limitless and free, under the lights, in Ebbets Field, watching the Dodgers, applauded by the fans.

Box Score 9

Brooklyn.	AB.	H.	O.	A.	Boston.	AB.	H.	O.	A.
Stanky, 2b	4	1	1	2	Holmes, rf	5	3	5	0
Robinson, 1b	5	0	6	1	Hopp, cf	3	0	2	0
Reese, ss	5	3	0	2	Rowell, lf	4	1	3	0
Furillo, cf	2	0	2	0	Elliott, 3b	5	0	0	1
Edwards, c	3	0	9	0	Torgeson, 1b	3	1	4	0
Bragan, c	0	0	2	0	Masi, c	1	1	6	0
Walker, rf	4	0	1	0	Ryan, 2b	4	0	2	2
Lund, lf	2	0	6	0	Culler, ss	4	2	4	2
Jorgensen, 3b	4	2	0	2	Spahn, p	2	0	1	1
Branca, p	2	0	0	0					
*Lavagetto	1	0	0	0	Totals	31	8	27	6
Hatten, p	0	0	0	1					
†Miksis	1	0	0	0					
Behrman, p	0	0	0	0					
Totals	33	6	27	8					

```
Boston   .................... 0 0 0   1 2 0   1 0 0—4
Brooklyn .................... 0 0 0   0 0 0   0 0 0—0
```

*Batted for Branca in seventh. †Batted for Hatten in eighth. R—Holmes, Rowell, Torgeson 2. E—Rowell. RBI—Culler, Masi 2. 2B—Reese, Torgeson, Masi. DP—Spahn and Masi. BB—Spahn 6. Branca 5. Hatten 1. SO—Spahn 5, Branca 7. Hatten 1, Behrman 1. Hits—Branca 5 in 7. Hatten 0 in 1. WP—Spahn. Loser—Branca. Umpires—Pinelli, Robb and Gore. Attendance—34,123.

51

It was a night game with the Braves. Burke was where he always sat near the dugout. Barber and Desmond were in the broadcast booth. The Dodger Sym-Phony was marching back and forth. Hilda Chester was ringing her cowbell. Eddie Bataan was blowing his whistle. Everything's in place, Burke thought, all the way it should be.

The Braves went down in order in the top of the first. Stanky led off for the Dodgers in the bottom of the first and singled to left against Johnny Sain. Robinson was up next. Cash slipped into the seat next to Burke.

'Where's the girl?' Cash said.

'My place,' Burke said.

'She all right?'

Burke nodded.

'She gonna stay with you?' Cash said.

Burke nodded again. Cash was silent.

'I'm leaving town,' Cash said.

'Where you going?' Burke said.

'L.A.,' Cash said. 'Lotta work out there.'

'Your kind of work?' Burke said.

'Yeah.'

They both watched Robinson foul off a curve ball.

'You turned out to be a pretty good guy,' Burke said.

'Funny how that happens,' Cash said.

Robinson took ball one.

'Good luck in L.A.,' Burke said.

Cash nodded.

Robinson swung and missed for strike two.

'Good luck with the girl,' Cash said.

Burke nodded.

Sain came inside to Robinson with a curveball that didn't break the way it was supposed to. It hit Robinson in the rib cage. Burke knew it wasn't intentional. You didn't hit somebody with a pitch when you had them down in the count 1–2. Without glancing at Sain he trotted down to first. He showed no sign that it hurt.

'I left you a little going-away present,' Cash said.

He handed Burke the next day's early edition of *The Daily News*. Burke looked at him silently for a moment.

'Page three,' Cash said.

'I'll take a look,' Burke said.

Reese came to the plate with two on and no outs. The excitement at Ebbets Field was palpable. Cash stood.

'See you around,' Cash said.

'Yeah,' Burke said. 'You ever need anything…'

'Sure,' Cash said.

He paused for a moment, then nodded his head at Burke and turned and walked up the steps and into the runway. On the first pitch from Sain, Reese hit into a double play. Carl Furillo fouled out to Bama Rowell in left.

Burke opened the tabloid to page 3. The headline read MURDER ON THE WEST SIDE. There was a picture of a man lying facedown on a flat surface. The lead paragraph began, 'Alleged West Side mobster Gennaro Paglia was found shot to death last night, in the men's room of a midtown restaurant.' Burke glanced back at the runway. But Cash was gone. Burke looked at the empty runway for a long minute, then folded the paper without reading further. Bob Elliott led off the top of the second.

52

Jackie was wearing a gray tweed topcoat with raglan sleeves and a military collar, turned up. It was two weeks to Christmas and snowing. Not a heavy snow, big flakes that came softly and were very white where they landed on Jackie's bare head. Burke wore a trench coat. He too was bareheaded, and between the two men, Lauren wore a camel's hair coat with a scarf over her hair.

They were standing near the statue of Prometheus, looking down at the ice skaters.

'Mr Rickey says I'm on my own next year,' Jackie said.

Burke nodded, looking at the skaters.

'And I'm out of work,' Burke said.

Lauren glanced carefully at each man, then back at the skaters. She didn't speak. The skaters were moving to 'Beautiful Ohio,' which Burke thought was probably a waltz. Burke had his arm around Lauren. Jackie stood on the other side of her, not touching.

'Well,' Jackie said, 'you won't miss the travel.'

'No,' Burke said. 'I won't.'

He looked at Robinson over Lauren's head. Robinson looked back at him. They were silent for a time. Lauren looked up at both of them again and still said nothing. The skaters moved softly below street level, on the dark ice, in the comforting snow, under the Christmas glitter, with Rockefeller Center rising above them into the snowfall. The music stopped for a moment, then returned. 'Beautiful Ohio' was replaced by 'Blue Danube.'

'I couldn't have made it,' Jackie said to Burke, 'without you.'

'Me either,' Burke said.

Lauren didn't speak. She kept her head against Burke's shoulder and her right arm around his waist. As the skaters circled below them, she put her left arm around Robinson's waist.

Robert B. Parker (1932–2010) has long been acknowledged as the dean of American crime fiction. His novels featuring the wise-cracking, street-smart Boston private-eye Spenser earned him a devoted following and reams of critical acclaim, typified by R.W.B. Lewis' comment, 'We are witnessing one of the great series in the history of the American detective story' (*The New York Times Book Review*).

Born and raised in Massachusetts, Parker attended Colby College in Maine, served with the Army in Korea, and then completed a Ph.D. in English at Boston University. He married his wife Joan in 1956; they raised two sons, David and Daniel. Together the Parkers founded Pearl Productions, a Boston-based independent film company named after their short-haired pointer, Pearl, who has also been featured in many of Parker's novels.

Robert B. Parker died in 2010 at the age of 77.